Reviews of *Cuz*, by Liz van der Laarse

A great read for adventure fans of intermediate and early teen levels. – Maria Gill (*Kids Books NZ*)

I'd recommend this for anyone who enjoys reading adventure stories. Ages 11+, and reluctant readers are also likely to be drawn in. – Sarah Forster (*The Sapling*)

A fast-paced read that is also the story of whanau and connection to whakapapa and tikanga while resonating with readers who feel they know little about their own place in the world. – Simie Simpson (*Magpies Vol 33, May 2018*)

First published by OneTree House Ltd, New Zealand

Text © Liz van der Laarse, 2018
978-0-473-42188-5

Cover design: dahlDESIGN
Printed: China

10 9 8 7 6   2 3 4 5 / 2

LIZ VAN DER LAARSE

OneTree
HOUSE

For Max,

with love and thanks for all the adventures – LV

ACKNOWLEDGEMENTS

I would like to thank my mates at Taipa for willingly sharing their knowledge: Carol and Les Hudson, Kylie Simeon, Sonia Peat, John Lee, Patrick Trenberth and of course, the late Tony Foster.

Thanks to my brother, Fraser Beer, for his help with things nautical.

Also, to the publishing team at OneTree House: Christine Dale and Jenny Nagle, for their enthusiasm and insightful guidance, and for believing in New Zealand writers and the importance of New Zealand children's literature for Kiwi kids. Finally, I wish to acknowledge the manākitanga of Māori for sharing their bushlore throughout Aotearoa New Zealand.

CHAPTER ONE

Over and over. His legs, his arms, his head, out of control. River thrust through the water, kicking out with his legs, gasping for air. The next wave crashed, taking him under, tangling his arms with bull kelp and smashing him into the sand. He scrambled up, pulling through the foam as the rip sucked at his legs, dragging him back towards the cold, grey sea.

River struggled up the beach, his feet sinking into the soggy sand, his breathing shallow and ragged. He threw himself face down beyond the high-tide mark and lay without moving. Useless. Salt water trickled down his back from his dreads.

He squinted at the sea. It looked as it had when he first went in. A light swell rolling in from the Tasman. Enough to make you want to try for a last body surf before winter. That set of dumpers had come out of nowhere.

River looked around for his hoodie and teeshirt. He turned towards home. His feet picked their way across the stones at the back of the beach, along the grass track through the gorse and lupins. He reached the main road and stopped. The sun glinted off a red Holden parked in his driveway. He frowned. Eh? Whose is that?

River crossed the road and walked up the path. The front door stood open. The voices came from the kitchen. His mother, Denise. And a man's voice. His father. He felt a quick stab of pain as he stepped inside, felt his legs shake. The man turned. River stared at the man who looked so like his father. Uncle Tau.

Tau's face broke into a huge grin. "Whoa, River. Look at you. Not a drowned rat but a drowned Rasta." He came over and pressed his nose to River's. "Good to see you, tama. Really good to see you." He looked hard at River's face. "How you been?"

"Yeah, good," River mumbled. He looked at the girl sitting at the kitchen table, her springy black curls and her smiling eyes.

"Kia ora, cuz. How's it?" she grinned.

He flicked his eyebrows. The last time he'd seen Huia was at their koro's unveiling. She'd been an annoying eight-year-old, poncing around knowing everything tikanga Maori. Making him feel even dumber than he already felt. And now here they were, both fourteen.

Denise spoke. "Tau and Huia are on their way back from Westport. They're going to stay the night."

"Yeah," said Tau, "I've been up to check out a new engine for my fishing trawler. Like what I saw too. Bloke says if I take the boat up there he'll drop the engine in for me. Take my old one as a trade-in."

River nodded. He sat down at the table next to Huia. They didn't look like cousins. He was as blonde as she was dark. But they shared the same serious brown eyes.

The talk was of how Nan had come in from the farm to live with Tau and his wife, of Denise's boutique at Punakaiki, River and Huia's first year at college. No one spoke of River's dad, Hemi.

"Hey River, take Huia down to the beach, eh?" Denise said. "Get some driftwood for a fire."

River raised his eyebrows at Huia. "Yeah, sure," she smiled.

Looking north or looking south, the beach faded into a haze.

"Far," said Huia, "this beach. No ends and no people. Has it even got a name?"

"Yeah. It's Fox River. Or near enough." River frowned. "Anyway, what about Riverton? It's not exactly the centre of the universe."

"It's my turangawaewae, River. Yours too, come to think of it." River looked down at the sand. Here we go again. "And anyway, there's Nan ..."

River glanced at her. "What about Nan?"

"She needs me around. Wants to pass on the stuff that she was taught ... by her tupuna. Taught me heaps. The real Maori ways."

River looked at her without speaking, then looked away. Yeah, yeah, rub it in. I know everything, you know nothing. Who was there to teach him? Does she think of that? He stopped by two massive logs beached in the sand. "This is our bonfire place. Head up the beach, eh? Heaps of wood up there."

Although the wind had a bite, the sun danced on the sand. The grains were coarse under their feet and between their toes. Logs and branches that had washed down the Fox River after rains, lay bleaching on the grey sands. They gathered smaller pieces in their arms and dragged branches along the beach, throwing the driftwood onto a stack.

"Anyone else live around here? You got any mates?" Huia asked.

"Course."

"So what do you fullas do?"

"I dunno. Hang at the beach. Fishing. Surfing. I go hunting with my mate, Dylan." He paused. "Do the garden for Mum."

"A bit of a hippy your mum, eh?"

"Yeah, I guess."

The fire was brilliant. Orange flames leapt upward against a clear black sky filled with stars. The warmth reached into their faces. River pulled his hood over his beanie, his long legs stretching out towards the fire. Tau and Huia sat on the sand with their backs against a large log. Tau's guitar rested on his legs while he strummed and sang softly. Huia joined in.

The waiata seemed to fit with the evening, the four of them alone on a beach with nothing but the stars and the fire, and the crash of the breakers. River heard his mother's voice and turned, surprised that she also knew the words. It was only he who didn't. He watched the flames send the words and notes spiralling until they too became part of the night sky. Tau put down the guitar. "I'm going for a fish. See what Tangaroa's got for us. You coming, River?"

Tau grabbed the bait bucket and handed a long rod to River. "You done much surf casting, tama?"

"Bit."

They baited up and waded into the icy shallows to cast their lines, retreating from the water to stand on the sand and wait. River's feet were numb and his rolled-up jeans clung wetly to his calves. The wind from the south froze his back and his hands were rigid on the rod, but there was a calmness in him as he stood with his uncle, just the two of them at the edge of the sea.

"What a beaut day for the drive home," said Tau the next morning, leaning across the top of the Holden. He tapped an unlit cigarette on the roof. "When the Coast turns on a day like this there's nothing like it. Look at that." They gazed at the Paparoa Range, its deep green forest a world of its own beneath a clear blue sky. "Nice part of the country all right."

He turned to River and Denise. "You know that new engine I was telling you about?" Denise nodded, pushing her fringe from her eyes. "Soon I'm going to have to take a run up the coast in the trawler to get it fitted. Around Easter. How 'bout I take River and Huia? They can crew for me. What d'ya reckon?" Tau turned to River, raising his eyebrows.

River looked up surprised. Eh? Crew for him? Does he know I've never been on a fishing boat?

"Ah . . . yeah," he mumbled. He looked back down at his boot, scuffing the shingle, then shot a look at Huia. He was sure she was laughing at him.

CHAPTER TWO

Riverton

River walked along the Riverton wharf carrying a chilly bin, his bag hitched over his shoulder, his mouth bulging with sticky marshmallow. Tau and Huia clomped in front, struggling under the weight of boxes and gear. River gazed ahead at the trawler. It was a real old timer. White hull, a mast at either end, wooden decks, blue wheelhouse sitting aft. A dinghy lashed to its roof caught the first rays of the early morning sun.

River took a deep breath, stepped on board the trawler and followed Huia into the wheelhouse. She pointed to a ladder leading down from the back corner. "That's the crew space, cuz. Shove your bag down there." She looked at his mouth and laughed. "How many Easter eggs did Nan sneak you?"

River backed down the narrow ladder to the cramped room and dropped his bag on one of the bunks. He listened to the waves slapping gently against the hull and breathed in the salty, fishy smell of the trawler. The knot in his stomach tightened.

Climbing back up to the wheelhouse, he saw Huia busily stowing tins and packets of food into the galley cupboards. And Tau swearing, his face screwed up as he struggled to attach the regulator onto the gas bottle.

River looked around the room. Everything in it had a function. The ship's wheel, dials of engine controls, what looked like an echo sounder, a radio transmitter, table and benches, gas stove, sink, and cupboards wherever there was space.

"Hey, River, bring us the other chilly bin from the wharf, will ya?" Huia called over her shoulder. River could hear Nan and Aunt Cheryl's lively chatter as they walked towards the trawler. He climbed on the boat's rail and pulled himself up onto the wharf.

"What do you think of our *Whetu*?" smiled Cheryl.

"Yeah, good," River replied. He felt Nan watching him and

he turned to look at her. Her eyes crinkled back. He wished he could ask her about his dad. Did she know where he was?

"You okay about this trip, tama?" Her eyes questioned him. He nodded. "Be good for you, boy. *Whetu* has been in our family for nearly forty years."

"Yeah?"

"She may be iti but she's brought home kōura for us year after year. She's like part of the whanau."

Tau came out on the deck. "What's this? You two down here this time of the morning."

Nan stuck her chin in the air. "Come to see my mokos off."

Tau laughed.

"How's it going?" asked Cheryl.

"Yeah, sweet. Time we were gone."

"There's bacon and egg pie in the chilly bin. Do you for lunch," said Cheryl.

"Yeah, yeah," said Tau, coming up onto the wharf and giving her a hug. "We've got heaps of kai. Kia ora for that. Ka kite, Mum," he said, kissing Nan. Tau turned and called out to Huia. "Leave that for now, girl. You'll have plenty of time later. We need to move."

"You make sure you use the sked, Tau. We'll be waiting." Cheryl looked hard at him.

"Well, don't be," he said. "There's a thousand and one things that can stop us from radioing. I don't need you worrying on top of that. We'll be fine, woman. It's a straightforward run up the coast in good weather."

"Don't worry what Dad says, Mum. I'll make him," said Huia, giving her mother a squeeze. Tau climbed down onto the trawler and went below. River heard the diesel grind over, revving noisily, then settle to a steady chug.

"I'll take care of the ropes," said Cheryl. "You two get on board. Ka kite ano."

River waved as the trawler moved away from the pilings. He stood beside Tau in the wheelhouse, watching as they moved past other fishing boats and old launches lining the Riverton estuary.

• • •

As they left the shelter of the bay and headed out into open waters River felt at once the roll of the sea. Tau turned to him. "She's not too bad a day out here. You're lucky. Some days this is not a good place to be, believe me."

River flicked his eyebrows. He tugged at the door, "Gonna grab some fresh air."

He pulled down his beanie against the wind and the salt spray and looked at the slow rolling waves making for the rock of the headlands. He watched gulls wheeling before the boat, shining white against the blues of the sky and sea. The land passed in a series of headlands and bays, the bush beyond clear in the bright sun.

The wheelhouse door slammed behind Tau. "I've left Huia at the wheel, but I'll take it around past Puysegur Point. See. There it is over there." River followed the direction of Tau's gaze off in the distance to a lighthouse on a long finger of land. "I wouldn't be bringing you two around Puysegur if the weather wasn't like this."

River looked at him. "Yeah?"

"You can get into mean strife here. When the Tasman Sea

is raging and meeting head-on with a storm sweeping up from Antarctica, look out. It's got the force to take a boat apart." Tau smiled at River's grim face and slapped him on the back. "But not today, tama. Today we're sweet as."

It was early evening when they entered Tamatea Dusky Sound and River saw at once how the name fitted. The stillness at the end of the day and the peace. A secret place at the end of the world, its dark water reflecting the dense forest of its islands and hidden coves.

Huia stood quietly beside him. "This place gets to you, eh?" she said. "You can feel its wairua." She saw the question in his eyes. "Its spirit, e."

River flushed. He moved towards the bow.

Tau took *Whetu* in slowly, past the little islands and bays, its chug, chug, chug breaking the silence, its bow breaking the mirror image of the bush.

The boat's engine quietened as they came round a headland into a cove and Tau cut back the revs. River heard the echo sounder beat out its tune and the noisy rattle of the chain dropping as they anchored well out in the bay. Then all was quiet. River looked up at the fence of mountains beyond, lightly touched with snow.

Tau came out of the wheelhouse. "Special place, eh tama?" They stood in silence for a moment and then Tau turned away. "We'll grab ourselves a feed of kutai to go with that kahawai I got. Give us a hand to get the dinghy off the wheelhouse roof. You can row."

River wove the dinghy crookedly across the water to a black rock. "Bring it in close so's I can lean over and grab them. You too, Huia." The clunking of mussels in the bucket became muffled as the pile grew. "That's enough. Always leave plenty for the next fulla." River shored the dinghy on the gravelly beach and a cloud of namu enveloped him, the sandflies hovering in his hair, his ears, his mouth.

Tucked into the headland, their fire burned strongly, keeping them warm as night settled. A huge moon hung in the sky, its reflection coming to them across the water. River felt his shoulders relax and he smiled. This is going to be all right, this trip.

On the wire rack, Tau turned the fillets of kahawai and

knocked the mussels onto a plate as soon as they opened. "You got the bread, Huia?"

"Āe."

"Karakia, then get into it. I'll stick the billy on."

Huia looked to River. He shook his head, blushing. She looked surprised, then bowed her head to give thanks for their kai. Bread, butter, mussels and fish. River loved the smoky flavour through everything. Even in his mug of tea. He sat back against a log, looking at the fire, listening to the familiar call of the morepork.

"Lot of history in this place." Tau spoke quietly. "Back in the day, a group of Ngāti Mamoe fled up here from Preservation Inlet with Ngāi Tahu hot on their trail. There was a mean scrap. The Ngāti Mamoe got wasted." He paused to light his rollie. "Later on, Captain Cook hung out in the Sounds giving the crew a rest after their time at sea. Then came the sealers ripping off our kai moana for the fat cats in Europe . . . after them, the whalers doing the same. They all came and they all went.

"And Tamatea was left to herself. The mountains keep

people out from the east and the sea keeps them out from the west and the south. Lucky it's only Coasters north of here, eh River, 'cause they don't move out of their backyard."

River grinned at him.

CHAPTER THREE

"Hey, River, hurry up, will ya." River blinked as Huia shoved a steaming mug of tea in his face. "Get this down you. We're on our way." He grabbed hold of it before she turned and scrambled up the ladder. The anchor chain chattered with the whirr of the winch and the diesel fired up.

Tau looked over his shoulder as River climbed into the wheelhouse.

"Morena, tama." River stood beside him at the wheel and peered at the day. The sky was clear but the early morning sun was still trapped behind the cold mountains.

"The wind's come up a bit," said Tau. "Won't be as good a day as yesterday."

Huia stopped banging pots around on the cooker. "Dad, you forgot to do the sked last night."

"I didn't forget. I just don't want your mum expecting me to call in every day. I'll do it tonight."

"Where we going to be tonight?" Huia asked.

"We're making for Milford. Should get there before it's dark."

"Milford Sound. It's beautiful, isn't it?" said Huia. She put the frying pan on the ring. "Make the toast, River."

"Don't be such a bossy cow," laughed Tau. They cooked and ate while *Whetu* nosed through the calm waters of Tamatea Dusky Sound. As they approached the last headland, Tau turned to them. "Bit of a different story out there. But not too bad."

Whetu butted out into the choppy swell of the Tasman. River watched in silence as the rolling waves crashed against the granite cliffs, white foam swirling, spray hurling to the sky. A gannet wheeled high above before dropping like a pencil.

They made their way up the coast, into the world of seals hunting amongst the bull kelp and dolphins planing alongside the trawler. Now and then the cliffs were broken by the entrance to a bay and they glimpsed the calm waters inside.

River and Huia took turns at the wheel, keeping the trawler on course while the sea slopped around it. River sniffed the air in the wheelhouse and asked, "Does it smell gassy in here to you?"

"This old-timer stinks of everything," Huia replied.

Tau joined them in the wheelhouse sometimes, keeping an eye on their progress and asking for cups of tea. "You two have a break. I'll take over."

"Come up the bow, River. See if the aihe are back." She saw his puzzled frown. "Dolphins, you goose," she smiled.

As soon as River stepped outside the wheelhouse cold wind and salt spray whipped his face. He walked unevenly, holding onto the top rail as he made his way along the deck to where Huia was hanging over the side.

"Look, cuz. Nga aihe. They're staying with us."

Tau smiled as he watched the cousins. "This was a good thing to do," he murmured, feeling in his pocket for his smokes. "Hemi should be here himself, the idiot."

Tau flicked his lighter.

Boom!

A whoosh of flame blew the wheelhouse apart, blasting Huia over the side and into the sea. River flew sideways, hitting the rail and tumbling to the deck. He stared open-mouthed at the raging fire. His heart thudded. Tau was in there. Inside the roaring flames. "Tau-au!" he screamed.

Grabbing the rail, River hauled himself upright. His eyes raked the choppy water. "Huia!" He saw her disappear in the waves. "No-o!" Her curly black hair bobbed up again. "Huia! Grab onto something!"

A deafening roar filled the air. River spun around, his eyes wide. The fire crashed to the engine-room below. "T-au-au!" The heat of the flames scorched his face. There was nothing he could do. He leapt.

River hit the freezing water, plummeting beneath, his hoodie and jeans dragging him deeper. His arms struggled against the weight of his sleeves as he struck upwards. His mouth gasped for air but the waves fell on him, taking him down. His skull ached with cold as the icy water closed over. River pulled at his heavy legs, fighting to keep his head above the choppy sea. He looked back.

Flames leapt and roared from bow to stern.

"Tau . . . !"

His stomach retched. Waves swamped over his face, choking him. Spluttering and coughing, River grabbed a broken board bobbing in the water. With trembling hands, he hauled himself on top and looked around wildly.

"Huia! Where are you? Huia?" He saw something moving. Something red. The swell rose, blocking it from sight. There. Again. Her arm, her red sleeve, waving. River raised his arm, his yell erupting. "Huia, over here!" He saw her head, her face turning to him. "Hold on. I'm coming!" River kicked towards her. Huia screamed at him but her words were eaten by the rage of the fire. River saw the name her mouth shouted and he stopped, unable to speak.

Gripping the lid of a chilly bin, she thrashed her way across to him. "Dad!" she screamed. "Have you s-seen Dad?" Her eyes tore at him.

"No . . . I . . . " Huia saw the horror in his face.

"River? Ha-ave you?" she shouted, her teeth chattering.

"The wheelhouse . . . " He looked at her helplessly. "It just exploded . . . he's . . . "

Huia stared at him, tears welling in her eyes. "No." River swallowed. She shook her head. "That's not true. We n-need to f-find him." She turned and kicked off strongly towards *Whetu*. "Dad! Dad!" River caught her. She struggled to free herself. "I'm g-going to f-find Dad."

River grabbed her arm hard. "Huia, he's gone. I saw it blow up . . . he couldn't still be alive. He couldn't be." He shivered against the tremors racking his body.

"No . . . n-no . . . you're wrong . . . " Huia shook her head, staring at the burning boat. "I'm not l-leaving him . . . "

A wave smashed down, twisting and tumbling them apart. The chilly bin lid shot out from Huia's grasp and she sank beneath the surface.

"Huia!"

Her curls floated down, down. River grabbed for her but she was gone, beneath the slapping waves. He stared stunned at the empty patch of water.

Suddenly her head bobbed from the sea. River grabbed her red jacket. He hooked under her arm and hauled her up, onto the board with him. She shook uncontrollably. "I'm n-not leaving h-him."

"Huia, he's dead . . . we have to go."

She looked at him, her eyes crazed, her black hair plastered to her blotched face.

"He can't be . . . "

River kept his arm tight across her shivering back. Cold ate into him, invading his bones. "You've gotta come . . . we'll freeze to death in this water. Tau wouldn't want you to stay. He wouldn't want you to die with him."

His knuckles white, River turned the two of them towards the cliffs.

At first her wail came softly, and then grew, reaching out for Tau. Huia looked wildly for nga aihe, the dolphins.

"Are nga aihe w-with Dad? Look, River . . . c-can you see?"

Sobbing, tears streaming, Huia slowly began to kick as if in a dream. River looked at Huia's blue face. He felt the chill of her body. Waves sloshed his shouting mouth. "Kick, Huia, kick."

Before them towered stark granite cliffs. Waves crashed over the gritty rock at their base. River searched for a place where the spray wasn't flying skywards, where the waves didn't meet the cliffs head-on, kicking out as the swell picked them up and little by little carried them in.

"There." He turned their board towards a small cove. They kicked out, rising and falling with the swell. River turned, his eyes wide, as a wave peaked behind them, crashing, taking them down. Over and over in the kelp Huia churned, desperate to breathe. Their board popped out of the water and they hit the stones, their arms flying. The next wave washed them up the stony beach, and then retreated, leaving them spluttering and coughing on the shore.

CHAPTER FOUR

River turned to look at Huia. She was curled like a snail, her eyes closed tight. Wet hair dripped down her face. Her soggy jacket and trackies clung to her shivering body. In her hand she clutched one of her trainers.

He jumped up, his eyes searching for Tau clinging to a piece of *Whetu* in the choppy water. But his heart knew the truth and his tears brimmed over. Huia staggered to her feet, her eyes wildly raking the white caps, the troughs and the wreckage.

"He's out there!" she cried.

River said nothing. He stared out to sea. How could life

change in a single moment? One minute everything was good as and the next Tau was gone.

Huia sobbed beside him, her face streaked with tears. He watched her walk down towards the water. She stood ankle deep in the tumbling stones, her wet curls plastered to her back, her eyes on the waves. Her soft moaning filled him with sadness.

His eyes searched the length of the beach, looking for Tau washed ashore. He looked to the stark rocky headlands closing off both ends of the cove, then turned around.

River gasped. Behind him, a vast forest stretched forever to a fortress of distant mountains.

Huia's wailing brought him back. She turned to him, sobbing. "I've . . . pleaded with Tangaroa . . . to give Dad back to us. He belongs to us. Mum . . . Nan . . . and me."

River led Huia to a long crevice in the cliffs, filled with sunlight. The sun fell on their heads as they huddled inside, their arms wrapped around their knees. Warmth radiated from the rock walls. River looked out at the cove seeing nothing, feeling Huia's body trembling beside him.

"Give us your jacket, Huia." She looked at him with dull

eyes. "I'll wring it out." He found a large boulder to shelter him from the wind coming off the sea and squeezed the water from the polar fleece. He wrung out his hoodie and his jeans, shuddering at their cold clamminess as he pulled them back on.

When he handed Huia her red jacket he saw she'd wrung out her teeshirt and track-pants. She murmured her thanks and turned to lie on her stomach, her head on her arms.

River heaped the sun-warmed shingle on top of her, then lay down and covered himself. His mind numb, he lay waiting for his shivering to cease, to feel his hands and feet once more.

The sun moved on leaving their cave in shadow. Huia mumbled into her forearms.

"What?" River grunted.

"I need to find Dad."

They stood at the head of the beach hugging themselves tightly against the wind. A cloud of smoke hung over the charred hull of the trawler. Remnants of *Whetu* littered the beach and the rocks below the headlands.

Huia walked away, shakily picking her way over the stones,

stopping at the wreckage, moving on. River watched her go. He climbed up on the rocky shelf jutting out into the choppy sea. Dodging the flying spray, he searched for Tau among the kelp surging in the channels. Huia's other trainer floated in a rock pool. As he bent to fish it out he saw something red and black between two boulders. His heart thumped. Tau's bush shirt.

River stared at the tattered remains of the Swanndri. He bowed his head. He knew Tau was dead. Had known the moment the wheelhouse blew apart. He lifted the scorched shirt from the rock and held it gently in his hands.

He looked up, searching for his cousin. The sun had dropped behind the far headland, leaving half the beach in shade. He squinted at the shadows. Huia stepped out from a flax bush and River called her name. He clambered down onto the beach to where she waited for him. Her eyes stayed on his face.

River stopped before her. He brought Tau's shirt and her shoe from behind his back. With a cry, she snatched the shirt from his hands and clutched it to her heart. Huia's voice rose from deep inside her as she walked down to the waves lapping the stones. Her karakia floated out over the water. River stood next to her, his hands hanging at his sides.

The wind had dropped but the shadows chilled their damp clothes. River led Huia back to the crevice. She lay curled on her side, the checked cloth clutched tightly to her. River looked at her blotchy face, her blue lips. He covered her with warm shingle. Her sobbing slowed, grew quieter and she fell into an exhausted sleep.

River looked towards the red horizon. When would someone come looking for them? Swallowing against the dryness of this throat, he stared at Huia, asleep, Tau's shirt loose in her hands. He had to stay. In the morning he'd find a stream. Somewhere in the forest.

River smoothed driftwood and loose rocks out of the way and lay down on the shingle, heaping it over his body. He shut his eyes and saw Tau, head back, laughing with Huia. And Tau again, serious this time, his face lit by the flames of their Tamatea fire. And now he was gone. Out of their lives. Like Hemi, his dad.

• • •

A violent shiver jerked River awake. Hunger twisted like a knife in his stomach, his head ached from thirst. He looked over at Huia's face, closed, sad even in her sleep. Stepping out of the crevice into the cold air of the dawn, he breathed in the tang of salt and seaweed. He turned away from the sea, to the east and the strand of light sky hovering above the mountains.

River waited for the day. Maybe the search for the missing trawler had already started. He heard Huia stirring. Watched her eyes open and then fill with despair. River looked down at his hands. When he looked up, she was watching him.

"Huia, we've got to have water. I'm going to find us a stream. I won't go far, eh?" Huia nodded and closed her eyes.

Walking along the high-tide mark below the driftwood, River searched the cove in the grey light, his heart heavy. His eyes scoured the debris washed up with the night tide, looking for Tau. The cold air reached into him, and he pulled his hood up over his head. An empty bottle lay stranded in the seaweed. Another rolled in the tide. Picking them up, he walked to the end of the cove and then turned towards the dark forest.

At once the beech trees closed around him. River looked

back towards the harakeke at the edge of the forest, their stalks silhouetted against the morning sky. He trampled ferns and clambered over moss-covered logs as he moved deeper into the bush. Branches and fronds broke beneath his feet. He stopped to listen for the sounds of water tumbling in a stream but heard only the birds and a fresh wind rustling the leaves.

River crashed on through the ponga and saplings. He slowed to catch his breath and knew he was climbing. Up and out of the valley. Away from Huia. He leaned against the trunk of a tall beech and sighed. "I have to go back."

His head throbbed as he smashed his way down to the cove, jumping off banks and sliding in the humus. Orange beech leaves littered the forest floor. Pushing through the harakeke, River saw the wind had come up, chopping the water and tipping the waves with white foam.

He stopped. *Whetu* was gone.

He ran to the line of driftwood and searched the sea. Nothing remained. The trawler had sunk beneath the bristling water. His throat thickened. Did Huia know? River saw her then. Combing the rocky shelf, looking for Tau, wearing his burnt and torn Swanndri over her clothes. He stood and watched before walking down to her. Huia looked up as he approached, dragging her hair from her face and shaking her head.

"*Whetu*'s sunk." River called. "The waves've swamped her."

She nodded. "I know."

"How are they going to find us now? How will they know we're here?"

Her eyes widened as she stared at him. She turned away to the empty sea.

"What's today, Huia?"

" . . . Wednesday."

"When were we gonna get to Westport?"

"Thursday. Thursday night."

"No one will look 'til Friday . . . "

"Maybe . . . not even then," Huia said quietly.

River stared at her. "What d'ya mean?" Huia didn't answer. "Would your mum have done anything . . . when she didn't hear from Tau last night?"

Huia's eyes swam with tears. "You heard Dad. It was all, Stop worrying about me, She'll be right." Huia wiped her eyes with her sleeve. "By the time they start looking . . . "

River spoke slowly. "We could be anywhere . . . "

"Yes." She turned to look out to sea. "Crayfishing stops during moulting. There'll be no trawlers around."

"The spotter planes will see us."

"Yeah? They've got the whole of the West Coast to search, River."

CHAPTER FIVE

For a long time neither spoke.

River looked at waves bashing the rocks and sucking down through the mussels. "Mussels . . . "

Huia shook her head slowly. "We can't eat from the sea, cuz." She saw the look of confusion on River's face. "It's tapu now."

"Eh?"

"Dad's still out there." She looked at him steadily. "We can get food from the forest."

He stared at her. He had to respect Tau. He knew that. But he was starving.

"Like what?"

"You'll see."

River watched Huia climb down from the rocky shelf and thread through the battered flax towards the bush. She'd better know what she was on about. What was she going to do? Stick a pig? He picked up a rock and chucked it against the cliff. A small avalanche of stones fell to the beach. River stumped after her.

Sunlight filtered through the canopy of branches, making pools of light on the forest floor and shining on the greens of the leaves. Huia wove through the ferns. River followed, the humus soft beneath his shoes. They hauled themselves up through the towering beech trees beyond the cove. River thought of the mussels clinging to the rocks. "So what's to eat, Huia?"

"Berries . . . it's autumn."

"Berries?" He groaned. Huia said nothing and they trudged on. "How come you know this stuff, anyway?"

"Nan. She's been teaching me since I was a baby. She doesn't want the knowledge lost . . . a walk with her takes forever . . .

showing me, asking me questions to see if I get it . . . Koro too, when he was alive. You remember him?"

"Not much." River paused. "Just the warm smell of that old brown cardie he used to wear. Always with a few lollies in the pocket."

"Ae," she said with a smile, "I remember that." Huia stopped. She stared straight ahead. "How could Dad be dead? How can you make yourself believe something like that?" She turned to look at him. River shrugged helplessly before dropping his eyes. "I have to keep hoping, River." River swallowed.

Their calves aching, they climbed up through the forest, kicking into the dirt and grabbing hold of scratchy fern fronds until they reached a ridge. Huia sat down heavily on a broken branch, drawing in deep breaths. "We should be staying with Dad. I feel bad leaving him down there."

River stared at her. "Eh? We can't help it. We'll go back soon. I gotta eat something, Huia." He turned away from her tear-filled eyes.

Huia led the way along the ridge, her eyes searching the shrubs and vines. River saw the way her shoulders sagged and remembered how out of it he'd been when he got to about eleven and finally figured his dad was never coming back. How nothing had touched him.

"Look, River. Down through the trees. A tōtara. It'll have berries."

They twisted through the beech trees, skidding on the leaf litter to the flaky tōtara below. Beneath it, tiny red berries lay scattered on the humus. River turned to Huia. "Is that only how big they are? You're joking, eh?"

Huia ignored him as she picked berries from the branches, biting off their red flesh and throwing their grey seeds away. River shoved handfuls of berries into his mouth, seeds and all, trying to fill the aching emptiness of his stomach.

"That's nowhere near enough. It's like eating nothing." He looked down at the ground. "When can we eat from the sea?"

"When . . . " Huia swallowed.

River looked away up through the trees. He didn't want to find Tau's body lying on the shore. But he knew the whanau would want Tau back. He could bury him with stones on the beach until they were rescued. Huia could say a prayer and then he could eat. Have a feed of mussels. Catch fish. Eat seaweed if he had to.

"River . . . "

He turned. "Yeah?"

Huia was sitting on a crown fern, her shoulders slumped. "I'm had it." She looked up at him, her eyes filled with sadness. "Let's go back down from here. We'll come out on the beach, eh?"

He nodded slowly. "Yeah . . . guess."

"I wanna go back to Dad. We can find a stream on the way down."

River sighed. "I've already looked down there."

He followed Huia as they slid down through the forest. He watched her stumble, exhausted, clamber heavily over logs, slither out of control on the carpet of dry leaves.

"How . . . much further . . . River?" she panted.

"Dunno. It's different to where we went up."

Huia stopped.

"Wa's up?" River slipped down to stand beside her. The ground dropped away, carved out by beech trees that had fallen, pulling their massive roots with them. Their huge trunks rotted at the bottom of the cliff. Huia sat down, hugging her legs to her chest. She dropped her head to her knees. Her black curls shrouded her shaking shoulders.

River stood near the edge of the overhang. "We can get down there, Huia. There's heaps of roots to hold on to. We can boot our feet into the bank as we go." He watched Huia, waiting for her. "We'll be sweet. True."

River went first. Backing down the cliff, testing roots before trusting them, kicking his shoes into the soft earth to make holds. He guided Huia step by step, telling her where to put her hands and feet. Silently, she did what he said. River looked down. They were nearly halfway.

"River!" He spun around. Huia slithered past him, her fingers desperately scrabbling in the dirt. "Stop me!"

"Grab on to something! Quick!" he yelled, watching helplessly as she tumbled, falling to the debris of mud and rotten wood below.

"Huia!"

CHAPTER SIX

Huia's cries of pain filled the air. River jolted down the slip, grabbing at roots, booting his feet into the dirt. He dropped to where Huia lay, her hand pressed to her left side. "My . . . ribs," she moaned, her eyes squeezed tight. "It hurts . . . to breathe." River knelt beside her. "Don't . . . don't touch me."

River swallowed. "Are you winded?"

She shrugged her shoulders. "Ow!"

He looked at her lying among the clods of damp earth and rotting roots. "You can't stay here. It's all wet. You're gonna have to move."

"Not yet," she whispered through pale lips and River saw how scared she was.

"Yeah, but soon."

He pushed through the saplings to a huge red beech tree. Dry leaf litter lay in thick piles between its buttresses. "It's better over here." He walked back to Huia. "You okay to move?"

"No . . . course I'm not." She sighed. "But . . . " Huia looked up at River. "Help me, cuz."

He slid his arm around her and she screamed. He stopped and waited. "Okay?" She nodded slowly. "Lean on me, eh? It's gonna hurt." Huia cried out as River helped her up. She winced with each short breath, each step. He lowered her gently within the buttresses. Grimacing, she leaned back against the foot of the tree and closed her eyes.

River stood for a long time looking at her lying there. If she'd cracked a rib, it'd be days before she could walk. Like that guy in the first fifteen. That was him gone for the rest of the season. He groaned.

"Go look for some berries . . . water . . . I'll be right. I just want . . . to lie here." She opened her eyes. River sighed and grabbed the water bottles. He marched through the trees, snapping off the ends of branches and muttering to himself. As if things weren't bad enough. They were stuck here now. He booted the humus with each step.

Eventually, he stopped to listen.

In the quiet of the forest, he heard water gurgling. A small stream trickled among the ferns. River slid a bottle beneath the surface and gulped down its icy water.

"Ho-o, that's cold." He drained a second bottle. More slowly this time. River filled their bottles and followed his trail of broken branches back, stopping to cram his pockets with red berries hanging from a vine.

Huia lay still. River stared at her drawn face. A shiver of fear snaked down his back. "Found us a stream," he said, handing her a water bottle. He took a handful of berries from his pocket. "These any good?"

Huia nodded. She drained the bottle and wiped her mouth. "Ae. They're kareao. Supplejack."

River put one in his mouth. It tasted like nothing. He

spat out the stone. "Berries are useless, Huia. They don't do anything like fill you up."

"Just leave it out, will ya? I don't need you going on as well."

River turned away. "Anyway, we're gonna have to stay here tonight. I'm gonna make us a tent."

He poked one end of a long branch through a fork in the tree behind Huia, and propped the other end through a tree in front. River rested branches of beech against his ridgepole and scrounged for fern fronds to weave through, filling in the sides.

"River?"

"Yeah?"

"Go down to the cove, eh?" Her voice broke. "Look for Dad."

"Yeah . . . yeah . . . all right . . . I need to finish this first."

River clambered down through the forest, keeping the afternoon sun in front of him. He heard the waves crashing and the cries of the seagulls, smelt the salt air as he jolted through the trees. Soon he'd see the flax guarding the bush at the back of the cove.

The forest grew lighter and River stepped out into the open. He stood on rock. On the top of cliffs of granite stretching away to the north and to the south. As far as he could see. His eyes dropped to the waves smashing on the rocks below. Eh? There's gotta be some mistake.

River looked up and down the coast again. Either way, the cliffs disappeared in the distant haze. Hiding their cove. And with it, Tau.

He screamed at the sky. Grabbing a large rock he held it high above his head and hurled it, watching it smash to pieces on the rocks far below.

He turned to stare at the forest and the mountains rising behind him. Groaning, River dragged himself away and trudged up through the trees to Huia.

She frowned at him. "What d'ya mean?"

"The beach isn't down there," River paused, swallowing. "I dunno where it is."

"But . . . what about Dad?"

"I know . . . "

"But . . . " She stopped.

River looked straight at her. "Huia . . . I can't leave you . . . I'd get lost . . . " She looked away from him.

"Yeah, and then what?" River finished.

Huia's shoulders fell with her sigh.

CHAPTER SEVEN

A splash of rain woke River. It hit his forehead, trickled down the bridge of his nose, slid down his cheek. He swore to himself. He looked at Huia in the dark, listening to her breathing. She was finally asleep. Another raindrop trickled into his ear. He swore again, twisting his cold body away from the hunger aching in his belly.

It was dawn when River woke next. He felt the damp seeping beneath him. Shivering, he looked over at Huia. She was staring up at the roof of their shelter. She turned when she heard him move. "This sucks."

"You feel any better?" River asked.

Tears welled in Huia's eyes. "No . . . it hurts to breathe . . . I'm wet . . . and starving. Dad's . . . " She shook her head. "No one knows where we are . . . that we're even alive." Huia breathed raggedly. "And I need to go for a mimi . . . I don't know how . . . but I do know . . . you're not going to help me."

They lay there, not talking, listening to the drops of rain in the forest. River spoke. "My guts never stop aching. It's driving me crazy. What . . . what can we eat, Huia? "

"Look for miro berries, eh . . . for the namu . . . sandflies . . . they're eating me alive . . . the berries are bright pink."

"Eh?"

"Miro berries. Nan rubs them on her arms sometimes . . . when we're down at the river. Their oil keeps the namu away."

"Yeah, but what about food? What's for food?"

"By the stream . . . were there creepers like . . . skinny cabbage tree leaves?"

River shrugged. "I dunno."

"Have a look, eh? Kiekie have fruit . . . like sweet corn . . .

but smaller." River picked up the bottles and crawled out of the shelter. "Don't forget . . . look out for miro," Huia called.

"Yeah, yeah."

This morning the beech leaves glistened, and raindrops hung from the soft ferns and mosses. River sloshed through the humus. Moisture seeped into his shoes, freezing his feet. He hugged himself for warmth. Berries, he snorted. Fish and chips more like it. Nah, a pie. A steak and cheese pie. That'd do it.

Dropping down into the gully, River saw the creeper Huia had talked about. Inside the base of the leaves grew a long green fruit, tinged with a pinkish yellow. He broke them from their stalks and filled the bottles with water, his fingers stinging with the cold. He followed his trail of snapped branches back. Huia stood holding onto a tree, gasping for breath.

"Been for a mimi." She smiled at the kiekie fruit in his hands. "Ureure. It's real nice. Give us a hand, eh?" Huia leaned on River and he guided her, shuffling, back to the shelter. She lay back against the tree trunk, wincing until she caught her breath again. "Okay . . . break it open . . . we eat the insides."

River broke off the outer layer, offering the fruit to Huia. She bit into it. "M-mm . . . tumeke . . . try it."

River tasted its sweetness, its energy. He grinned at her. "That's more like it. Real food . . . almost." He ate the rest hungrily. And another. He reached for his third. "You reckon they'll be searching for us yet?"

"River . . . " She looked at him. "There's something else I thought of."

"What?"

"They'll be searching the sea."

River stared at her. "Eh?"

"They'll be looking for a trawler, won't they . . . not two kids in the forest." She swallowed. River kept his eyes on her face. Her words hung in the air between them.

CHAPTER EIGHT

River burst from their shelter and hurtled down through the bush to the top of the cliffs. He stared at the sea. That's where they'd be looking, all right. Out there. The Tasman Sea. There would be no help. No rescue.

He turned to the dark forest stretching to the humps of mountains in the far distance. The way home. He sighed. They'd never do it.

The sun broke through the morning mist. Through the beech trees, River saw a clearing fill with light. He pushed his way through to it and sat on a rock, staring at the ground. They had no choice. His shoulders slumped.

He felt the sun on his hair and raised his head to look around. It was better here. Warmer and drier. Open and flat. A good place for a hut. As River stood up to leave a shrub at the edge of the clearing caught his eye. Among its long leaves hung fat orange berries. He grabbed a handful and shoved them in his mouth. "Yuck." He tramped back up to Huia.

"Hey," he said, crawling into their fern tent. "I've . . . " He saw her red eyes. "Is it sore?"

"No . . . Dad . . . it's not right to leave him."

"It's not our fault."

"I know . . . but it's not right."

"When we get home . . . we'll make it right somehow," said River. "The whanau'll know what to do."

"Stay with me now, River . . . say a karakia with me . . . ask Tangaroa . . . to look after him . . ."

River looked at her, then nodded. Huia's prayers filled their shelter. Their waiata floated out into the beech trees, Huia's voice gasping for breath, River's faltering beside hers as he followed her words.

Huia leaned on her cousin as he helped her to the clearing he'd found. River paused by the shrub with the orange berries. "What are these?" he asked her.

Huia peered at them. "Don't know. Don't think we have them back home. Better not touch them."

"Eh?"

"Well, some things could be poisonous. You know that."

"I ate some."

"What?"

"I didn't think . . . Okay? I'm hungry."

Sighing, Huia shook her head as River helped her lie down. He sat next to her, letting the sun warm him, swiping at the sandflies hovering around his face.

"What are we going to do, River?"

"Don't have much choice. Stay here until you're better. Then . . . "

"What?"

"Set off home."

"How we gonna do that?"

"Walk to the mountains."

"Have you seen how far that is?"

"Yeah . . . "

Huia sighed. They both fell quiet.

River broke the silence. "Far, I'm too hungry to do anything. Let alone walk a hundred ks."

"Koro said the forest provides. If people look after the forest . . . then the forest will look after them."

River raised an eyebrow at her.

"Ae, but you've got to respect it, River . . . Respect its mauri."

"Its what?"

"Its life-force."

He looked away through the trees. He didn't want to say "what's that?" again. He gazed at the tall grey trunks of the beech, the vines dangling from their branches, the fresh, leafy saplings springing up from the ground. The forest did look like it had a life of its own. A world within itself.

Huia interrupted his thoughts. "You know . . . might be kōura in that stream . . ."

"Yeah?" River turned to her. "Those little crayfish things? How d'ya catch them?"

"Break off some manuka branches . . . lean them upside down in the water . . . kōura hide in the leaves."

He squashed a namu on his arm. "But I need a feed now . . ."

"Supplejack and kiekie. You know them." Huia paused. "Cabbage tree shoots . . . young shoots of toetoe . . . " River stood up. "Bring me kiekie leaves, eh? I'll have a go at weaving a hinaki."

River looked down at her, frowning.

"Hinaki. Eel trap, cuz."

River brought back stunted manuka branches from the top of the battered cliffs.

"Hey, tumeke," said Huia, blowing on her cold hands. "Tight and thick . . . good hiding places for kōura. Or so they think."

Taking the leafy branches through the forest to the stream, River pushed them down into the water, jamming some branches with rocks and sticking others tightly among the roots of overhanging shrubs. In the dark gully by the stream, he searched for kiekie, grabbing its fruit and long leaves to take back to Huia.

"Cuz . . . " she grinned. They bit into the fruit, eating quickly, leaving nothing.

"Not quite hamburger and chips. Or one of Mum's big toasted sandwiches," River said.

"Wonder what our mums are thinking, eh?"

They were both quiet and then River spoke softly. "They'll be going nuts."

CHAPTER NINE

Huia leaned over and picked up some blades of kiekie. Pain stabbed her chest. She leaned back against the log, catching her breath, and began to strip the leaves for her weaving. River got up and entered the forest, looking for branches and ferns to make a hut.

It was bigger than the last one but the basic design was the same. Like a tent. Either end of a long ridgepole was stuck where a low branch met the tree trunk. Fern fronds wove through leafy beech branches to make the sides. This time River made a wall for the back. For the front end, he used kiekie to tie three branches into a triangle which he filled with fern. But this wall could be moved away, like a door.

"Our whare iti," Huia smiled. She hugged her arms lightly across her chest. "We need a fire . . . I get so cold sitting around. My clothes aren't even properly dry yet."

"What did Nan teach you? She told me that story once. Which tree holds the seeds of fire?"

"Kaikōmako."

"Is it here?"

Huia squinted at the forest surrounding the clearing. "Dunno. Go and get heaps of different leaves . . . and I'll have a look."

River saw the forest was full of all kinds of plants. He collected thick and shiny leaves, ragged and fragile ones, others hairy and leathery. Huia picked out a soft leaf with zigzag edges.

"Is that kaiko . . . something?" River asked.

"Kaikōmako. Nah, this is māhoe. We need it too . . . it's the soft wood. Kaikōmako is the hard one."

"Did I get that?"

Huia held up leathery leaves shaped like a duck's feet. "Ae."

"Yeah? Awesome." He looked back into the forest. His smile disappeared. "Far, how am I going to find them again?"

"Take the two leaves with you, cuz. Māhoe's bark is white . . . look for that . . . the young kaikōmako plants are a crazy pile of thin-as branches . . . the mother tree will be near it. And grab some dry lichen too. Or dried leaves."

"Eh?"

"For fire starters."

River searched among the mossy trees, through tangles of vines and scratchy ferns. His eyes rested on an old grey tree. He grinned. It had the duck-feet leaves. River grabbed a broken branch wedged in the tree. By the edge of the clearing, a white-barked tree stood out against the greens. Māhoe.

"These them?" He held the two branches out to Huia.

Her blue fingers grasped the wood. "Ae, fulla." She grinned up at him. "Shove the māhoe tight against something. Make a groove in it with the kaikōmako." He pushed the stick against the māhoe branch. "Rub it back and forth . . . hard and quick." It skated off to the side. Shaking his stiff hands, he tried again. And again.

He huffed warm breath on his fingertips. "It needs a point."
He hunted around for a sharp stone and scraped away at the
end of the stick. "Give us the māhoe. You come and hold it,
eh? So it stays still." Huia knelt in front. Her arms stiff, she
held the wood tightly. River drew the stone sharply down its
length. And again, and again, until a groove was formed.

This time the stick stayed in. He pushed it faster, faster and
faster, faster and faster, faster, back and forth, back and forth
until his arms ached.

"River, the dust in the groove . . . that's it . . . that's what's
going to catch on fire."

He sniffed. Smoke. A little thread curled towards him.

"Look, Huia." He lay down by the māhoe branch, gently
waving his hand by the smouldering dust until a spark became
a tiny flame. Blowing softly, River placed a couple of dried
leaves over it, then the tiniest of twigs, fanning them alight.
He looked up, grinning. "How's that, cuz?"

"Awesome, River. Now we can cook stuff."

"Yeah . . . if we had something to cook."

• • •

Warmth from the fire reached into their bodies. River and Huia sat, saying little, watching the steam rise from their clothes. Huia struggled against the lump, raw in her throat. "We're so far away from everyone. So alone."

River stared at the fire. "We'll get going when you're strong enough to handle it."

In his mind, he saw the mountain ranges he'd seen from the cove, row after row. He picked up a fat branch and chucked it in the flames, sending sparks flying.

Huia gave him a startled look. "What's with you?"

"The way back. It's epic." River looked over at her. "You know anything 'bout where we are? Like, what's between Tamatea and Milford?"

"Lake Te Anau. Lake Manapouri." Her voice faltered. "A heap of wilderness between the coast and them. And mountains."

River groaned.

Huia took a breath. "If we walk towards our waka our tupuna will look over us," she said quietly.

He turned to her. "What are you on about?"

"The waka that we come from, River. Tākitimu. The Tākitimu Range. Our tupuna will guide us." She looked at him staring at her. "You'll see."

He frowned at the fire. Dad should've stayed . . . he should've taught me this stuff . . . I don't know nothing.

River heard his stomach rumble as he added skinny dry branches one at a time, watching the small flames take hold. Suddenly, he doubled over clutching his belly. Pain ripped through him.

"What's the matter?"

"My guts!" River rolled on to the ground. "I feel sick . . ." He tried to stagger up, but fell on his hands and knees, vomiting.

"Cuz!" Huia cried.

River crawled away and lay on his side. He dry retched, again and again, clutching his belly, his face flushed and shining with sweat.

He lay where he was until the retching had stopped. Even sips of water he couldn't keep down. As evening fell he crawled into their whare. All through the night he was woken by the pain in his gut and waves of nausea. Sweat drenched his teeshirt. Towards dawn he finally fell into a deep sleep.

River woke when he heard Huia stirring. He opened his eyes. She was watching him, a worried look on her face. "How do you feel?"

"Terrific . . . what do you think?"

Huia frowned.

"Nah, better than last night. But gutless as . . . I bet it was those orange berries I ate."

Huia spoke quietly. "You're lucky, cuz. It could have been a lot worse."

"This was bad enough." River paused, listening. "Is it raining?"

Huia nodded.

"The fire!" River wriggled out of the whare.

He poked the rain-pocked ash with a stick, stabbing and raking until he uncovered a faint glow. He nursed it with old cabbage tree leaves and dry twigs, fanning the embers into licks of flame, building the fire until it blazed.

They sat under the beech watching the dripping rain, swiping at the namu, waiting for the flames to warm them. River grimaced as a pang of hunger racked his body. He looked at Huia's weaving lying on the ground. "When's your eel trap gonna be ready?"

Huia grinned, holding up what looked like a woven cylinder, open at one end and narrowing to its base. "It is."

"Eh? How does that work?"

"Like this. See. The tuna, he can swim into the hinaki but he can't turn around and come back out."

"Cunning, cuz."

"Yeah, well, let's see if it works first. Put it where the water moves slowly, River. Like a hole. Or under a bank."

"You reckon there's eels in that stream?"

"Ae, now's the time they swim down-river and out to sea."

"Give it here. I'll give it a go."

River pushed himself up and walked gingerly through the forest carrying the hinaki. Now and then he stopped to rest, leaning against the solid trunk of a beech tree. He stepped into the water and made his way upstream, ducking beneath fern fronds and holding onto rocks as he caught his breath, feeling the water rush past his calves. He stopped and stood looking at a place where the stream had carved out a bend and the current flowed calmly. That's what Huia meant, eh? One side of the trap River tied to a submerged branch, and the other to a long root reaching into the water.

River dragged himself back to the fire and slumped to the ground. He saw Huia had managed to gather more wood. "You feel any better today?" he asked.

She nodded. "That's the thing about a fire, eh? It gives you hope. That things mightn't be so bad." They sat with their backs against the beech, their hands outstretched towards the flames. "I so wish our mums knew we were alive, River. And Nan."

He thought about Denise. Thought of her staring blankly through the kitchen window at the bush-clad hills of the Paparoa. Hemi gone and now . . . River looked over at Huia and then looked down at his hands. Looked at her again and took a breath. "Huia?"

"Yeah."

"You ever heard Tau and Cheryl talk about my dad? Where he is and stuff." River swallowed. "Why he left."

"I asked them once."

"Yeah?" River jolted. "What'd they say . . . ?" He heard the tightness in his voice.

"You really want to know?"

"Yes."

"They said that he and Denise were really young when you were born. Teenagers, eh. It was too much for Hemi to handle. Working long hours in the forestry while his mates were still hooning around. One day he just went. Jumped on a plane and went to Oz. They reckon he's too 'shamed to come back. Mum says it's not good enough. He's not grown up until he does."

"Does my mum know?"

"She must, I guess."

"She won't talk about it. Just gets upset and bites my head off . . . and then it's all, sorry, sorry . . . so I stopped asking."

"That's rough, cuz."

River shrugged and looked into the fire.

CHAPTER TEN

River walked slowly through the forest to the stream. He ached with hunger. He thought about how every day after school he couldn't wait to get off the bus and slather a fat slice of Denise's home-made bread with peanut butter and honey. Then rip open the fridge and down a glass of milk.

He snorted. That was sweet compared to this.

River needed both hands to pull up his manuka branches. His eyes searched for kōura glistening among the dripping leaves. "Come o-on." He slowed down, carefully folding back the leaves. "Don't give me that . . . "

River shoved the branches roughly back under the water. "Useless!"

He struggled upstream, fighting against the current. When he reached the hinaki, he waited under the hanging branches, watching to see if it moved before wading over to the trap. It lifted too easily, too lightly. Water poured out of the woven strips of kiekie. "What a great . . . fat . . . waste of time!" He dropped the hinaki back into the stream.

Head down, he trudged back through the forest. Huia looked at his empty hands. She let out a long sigh. River threw himself down by the fire. "Far, my guts ache so bad . . . "

"Mine too. Soon we'll be too weak to go anywhere."

"Yeah . . . tell me about it."

River raised his finger to his lips. He turned his head, listening, and stood up quietly. He crept into the forest, his feet slow and soft on the humus. Something scratched among the crown ferns. A brown bird like a kiwi scooted from the fronds. River grinned as he watched it scuttle away through the beech trees.

He walked back to Huia. "A weka!"

"They're protected . . ."

"Eh? We'll die if we don't eat. Anyway, didn't Koro tell us they'd eaten them on the Chathams that time him and my dad and your dad went over?"

"Yeah," Huia admitted, "he did tell me about hunting weka once . . . they are real curious . . . that's how you catch them . . . make them come nosing around."

"Well . . . ?" said River.

"Get kiekie leaves for my weaving, River. Get heaps, eh . . . we'll try to think of something."

They sat and stripped the leaves into long strands, Huia chatting on, pausing to catch her breath. "Koro told me this story . . . about when he and Dad and Hemi were out hunting wild sheep on the Chathams . . . they hadn't caught anything, eh, and it was too shame to go back empty-handed . . . A weka was tutuing around where they stopped for lunch . . . Koro told the boys how they could catch it . . . Koro hid in the toetoe with a noose to tighten around its neck . . . Hemi had to make the weka come towards the toetoe."

"How did he do that?"

"You know you can make that whistling noise with a bit

of grass?" She took a breath. "Was meant to make the weka think . . . it was a mate for him."

"Like this?" River held a strip of kiekie tight over his pursed lips and blew.

"Ae, that's the one. Weka are mean fighters. Dad had to waggle some little branches just behind the noose . . . so the weka would think there was another bird . . . in his territory."

"Did they get it?"

Huia started to laugh, clutching her side. "Ow . . . that hurts . . . they forgot about Dad's hay fever . . . just as the weka was getting close, the fluffy toetoe tickled Dad's nose, eh, and he sneezed. That weka was out of there . . . Hemi gave him heaps and Koro . . . he didn't stop laughing for a week, he reckoned."

"Let's do it."

They fiddled with the strips of kiekie until they had made a noose with a slipknot that tightened easily. The other end they fastened around a long skinny branch like a fishing rod.

"Get some berries to make the weka come back."

River pushed through the shrubs and vines until the bright

pink of miro berries caught his eye. He filled his pockets and walked back to Huia.

"Kia ora, cuz." She smeared the oily flesh over her face and hands to ward off the sandflies. "Drop berries near a place . . . where I can hide."

River laughed. "Your dad was right. You are a bossy cow." Huia bent her head, picked up the long strands of kiekie and began weaving.

"Aw, sorry, cuz. He only meant it as a joke."

"I know he did," Huia mumbled, her eyes wet.

"I'll find a good place for the berries. Then I'm going to check my kōura trap. And the hinaki."

Again the traps were empty. River stumbled through the water, holding onto boulders, shoving fern fronds out of his face. He dragged his feet back to their camp. He stopped, turning to lift his eyes to the distant mountains and sighed. If they didn't eat soon they'd never make it.

Huia lay beside the fire, her eyes closed. River crept up into the forest to where he'd scattered the miro berries. Eh? He turned right around, his eyes searching. His frown became a smile. River walked softly down through the crown fern.

"Hey, something's eaten our berries. D'you hear the weka?"

Huia slowly shook her head. "I fell asleep. But good, eh? That weka must still be around." She reached for her weaving.

River crept back to where he'd scattered the berries and hid within the buttresses of a beech. He waited, hugging himself against the cold. A skinny-legged robin hopped on his shoe, looking at him with its black bead eyes, its head cocked. Ferns rustled. Something scratched among the dead leaves. Very slowly he rolled his head around the trunk. He smiled slowly. The weka was back.

River walked down to Huia and stood in front of her, grinning. "It's on, cuz."

When dusk darkened the shadows of the forest, River helped Huia up to a clump of ponga. She settled behind them with her kiekie whistle. In her hand she carried a little bunch of manuka. River crouched next to her. He poked his rod through the dead fronds, its noose hanging ready.

They waited, shivering, listening. The wind breathed in the branches and then, a scuttling. River raised his eyebrows at

Huia. She lifted the blade to her lips and blew. The scuttling stopped. She whistled again. River could see the weka now, pausing and looking towards their hiding place.

Huia rustled the dry fern with her manuka brush. The weka came at the ponga, his head down, straight through the noose. River yanked it upwards, the noose tightening around its neck as River struggled to stand up.

"Got it!" The weka hung from the noose, its feet scrabbling in midair. Grabbing its head, River swung the bird around, hearing the crack as its neck broke. "Meat, cuz, meat!"

"We did it!"

Still grinning, River jabbed at the stream bank with a stick. He dug a bowl in the loose dirt and mixed in a little water from the stream. Pulling the weka into the hollow, he plastered its feathers with his mud. River carried the bird back to the campfire holding onto its feet. He called out to Huia. "This what you meant?"

"Ae, that'll do," Huia laughed. "Stick it on the embers." She covered the bird with small glowing chunks of burning wood.

"You reckon it'll work?" River asked.

"Dad did it with a chook . . . when we were camping out on the heads . . . Koro told him about it. The mud stops the meat from burning, eh."

"How long d'ya have to cook it for?"

Huia shrugged. "Hour? You save the guts for eel bait?"

"Yeah." He looked down at Huia. "Tau would be pretty proud of you, I reckon."

A faint smile crept on Huia's lips and then disappeared. "Hey," she said, turning away. "Made you this. Finished it this afternoon." She reached behind the log and held up a lopsided pikau, roughly woven from the kiekie leaves. "For the journey. The epic journey." She laughed.

"Kia ora, cuz." Smiling, River slipped on the backpack. "It'll fit heaps in there."

They sat watching the mud dry and fissure on their plastered bird. As they piled embers on the weka they smelt the whiffs of it cooking. River's stomach rumbled. "I can't wait any longer. Quick, say a karakia, Huia. Make it a short one though."

She laughed. "Hey, good for you, River." She bent her head to give thanks for their kai before she cracked open the casing.

The feathers came away in the dried mud. They tore at the meat, stuffing their mouths full. Juice ran down their chins as they sighed and grinned at each other.

"Tu . . . what is it?" laughed River.

"Tumeke."

"Yeah . . . tumeke, cuz."

CHAPTER ELEVEN

It was the cold that woke River. He dragged the bracken up over his shoulders and pulled his hood tight around his face.

Huia turned to him, "Let's go today. If we leave it longer it's just gonna get colder. Go now before there's snow in the mountains."

"You reckon you can?"

"Even if I can't go far . . . to start with . . . it still gets us closer to home."

"What about food?"

"Same as here. Catch birds. Eels. Berries and plants."

"Yeah. You're right." River stood up. "Let's get out of here."

Huia gathered the puku tawai, the beech fungus she'd collected to help start their fires on the journey. She placed it in River's pikau next to the ureure fruit, the leftover weka meat wrapped in kiekie leaves, and water bottles with sticks for corks. She had woven two straps for the hinaki and that became her pikau. Broken branches of kaikōmako and māhoe protruded from the top.

They stood and looked at their whare and the clearing that had been their home. Huia bent her head and River waited. "What was that karakia about?" he asked.

"Giving thanks for what we have been given by the forest and the stream and asking to be led back safely to the waka of our ancestors."

He looked at her, and stepped back, letting her lead, letting her walk in her own time. "What do you mean by that? Walking back to the waka of our ancestors?"

She stopped to answer, her words seeming to belong to the forest. "Like I said ... You and me, our whanau, trace our whakapapa back to the Tākitimu waka, eh? Tākitimu travelled down the east coasts of the North and the South Islands ... at different places, tupuna stayed and that became the whenua for those people . . . they say Tākitimu ran aground in the Waiau River . . . that its hull lies in the shadow of the mountains rising up from the plains, the Tākitimu Range . . . so I reckon if we walk back towards the waka of our iwi, our tupuna will keep an eye over us."

River looked at her closely. "Do you really believe that, Huia?"

"Ae. Koro and Nan always seemed pretty wise to me. They say our tupuna are around still. Guiding us."

Huia turned and began her slow walk up through the forest. River followed, thinking about what she'd said. He thought about the photos of the tupuna on the walls of the whare tupuna at the marae. Huia's marae and, she was right, it was his too. The hapu felt their tupuna's presence there. They were included in everything.

He looked around him. At the untouched world of the forest. Its wild beauty. Felt its life-force. Its mauri, Huia called it. Were their tupuna here? With them, in the wilderness?

• • •

Now and then the morning sun reached through the canopy of beech and warmed their faces as they began their eastern journey. River followed Huia, helping her clamber up the side of the mountain, listening to her sharp intake of breath, her panting, seeing her eyes screwed with pain.

"Your ribs?"

"Ae."

"You wanna stop?"

Huia shook her head. "You?"

"No," River said. He tramped behind her, his hunger gnawing like some kind of animal. Gnawing, growling. Never letting up.

He stumbled through the crown fern and scratchy ponga, grabbing onto saplings and booting into the mud and humus. On and on he climbed. His calves ached. Sweat dripped from his dreads.

River stopped to catch his breath. Far, this is only the beginning. Day after day it's gonna be like this. He peered up through the tall dark trunks of the beech trees. Huia sat resting on a rotting log, her shoulders sagging. "It's wet as . . . but there's nowhere else and I'm had it. Past had it even."

River grabbed hold of a branch to pull himself up a mossy bank. He plonked down next to her, puffing. "What've we . . . got to eat?"

Huia looked at him. "Better save it for lunch, eh? We haven't got much."

River sighed. "What would you eat, Huia . . . if you could eat anything . . . right now?"

"Don't, cuz. It only makes it worse."

He grunted. "You gonna make it to the top?"

She turned and looked River in the face. "I have to. Are you?"

He smiled, raising an eyebrow. "Is that a wero?"

Huia laughed. "Where did you learn that, Pakeha boy?"

"I've been to a powhiri," he laughed.

"Just the one, was it?" She smiled at him. He smiled too. "Just teasing, River, come on."

They struggled on up through the wet rainforest, clambering over fallen branches the size of tree-trunks, the moss soaking their clothes. Piwakawaka darted between the black kareao vines that looped the saplings and ferns growing among the giant beech trees. But River took no notice. He looked only at the ground as he hauled himself up the spur, every step an effort.

He caught up to where Huia stood with her arms wrapped around her ribs. "I didn't know . . . it would be . . . this hard," she panted.

"Yeah. I'm real gutless too." River bent over, placing his hands on his knees. He rubbed his sore calf muscles. Huia handed him a handful of orange berries she'd picked between the silvery blades of a kakaha. River grunted his thanks.

Huia's eyes searched for the open sky of the tops. "It's never-ending."

"You had enough for today?"

"No way. I'm gonna do this."

River kept closer to Huia, as they trudged on in silence, too breathless to talk. Eventually, he felt the air freshen and saw the beech trees had become stunted and deformed. "We're getting closer to the tops, cuz."

"About time, e."

As the ground began to flatten they threaded through the spiky shrubs of mountain beech. River's hair whipped his eyes as he looked to the sky. The sun shone directly overhead.

"We made it." River put his arm round Huia's shoulders.

"Cuz . . . you're sweaty as."

"Yeah, but I made it." He took his arm away. "You all right?

"Okay . . ." She placed her hands on her ribs. "Sore." She smiled at River. "I need a rest though . . . and a kai."

"Yeah. Me too. I'm starving."

CHAPTER TWELVE

They sat behind a clump of mountain beech to shelter from
the wind. Huia fanned her face with her hand. River passed her
a water bottle. "Not much left." He wiped the sweat beading
on his forehead. Huia brought out the last of the weka meat
from the pikau and gave River half. He wolfed it down.

"That's not going to do it," he sighed. "Not by a long shot."

"We have to keep the ureure for dinner or we'll have nothing to eat," Huia said.

River picked up a few stones and fired them one by one at
a nearby rock. He sighed again and got up.

"I'm gonna see what's over the other side."

He pushed through the tussock and stunted shrubs until the ridge began to drop away. River stood looking out over the forest. Mountain ridge after mountain ridge lined up before him, each clothed in deep dark green. In the distant blue haze rose the stark grey tops of the Tākitimu Range. Huia struggled up behind him. "Our waka."

"Look where it is, will you? So far away you can't hardly see it. How do we even know how to get there?" River stared at the sea of forest, counting the number of ridges to the Tākitimu Range. But they ran into one another, twisting and turning with black river valleys, merging and fading as they neared the mountains. He shook his head.

"We walk towards the mountains," Huia said.

"And when we're down in the creeks? Or in the forest . . . where the trees block out everything? What then?"

"We walk towards the morning sun."

River snorted. "There's no sun in those valleys." He shook his head again.

"What?" Huia asked.

"We'll never do it."

Huia kept looking at the journey ahead. "We can walk along the ridges that go east."

River snapped at her. "Yeah, and where there are no ridges going east we're going to have to climb up and down mountainsides. And there's heaps of those. Heaps."

Huia ignored him, her eyes on a dark valley twisting through the lumpy forest. "We can walk up the valleys the rivers are in."

"How do we know they're coming from the east? Rivers go all over the place."

Huia spoke slowly. "You know, from up here, it looks like a map . . . a 3D map. We know east is where the Tākitimu Mountains are . . . see that ridge here goes east." River looked to where she pointed. "So that ridge would be good to follow . . . start with that and go until it goes off in another direction."

"Yeah? And . . . then what?" River grumped.

"We look at the new 3D map in front of us. Look at what will take us east . . . and follow that."

River said nothing.

He turned away and went back to where his pikau lay on the ground. He dropped down next to it. They'd never make it. It was a joke to think that they could.

Huia walked back and sat down beside him. River turned around and lay on his stomach, his head on his forearm. He closed his eyes. Epic as. He heard Huia settle down to rest. He sighed.

"You ready?" Huia pushed herself off the ground and handed River his pikau. "Let's go." She walked through the dwarf-like trees towards the ridge she'd pointed out. The one heading east. River slung his pikau over his shoulder and followed, saying nothing.

With her hands on her ribs, she led him along on the stony ridge as it dipped and rose. River looked out over the forest as he walked, watching the sun move slowly towards where the sea lay out of sight. The West Coast. His home.

Suddenly, the ridge dropped away and became a spur to the stream below. Huia turned to River, raising her eyebrows.

"Yeah, well, if we go down here," he said, "we're still

heading east. Then, see that." He pointed. "That valley across the stream. Feeding into it. It's coming from the east too." Huia smiled to herself as she turned away.

Slowly they stumbled down through the mossy trees and clumps of kakaha, listening to the sounds of the stream rising to greet them until its roar filled the forest. River stepped through the last of the trees and stopped still. Before him a wide river rushed headlong around rocks, tumbling and cascading, its spray dancing high in the air.

Huia slumped to the jumble of river boulders. River looked down at her. "This is how it is, Huia. We don't have a choice."

CHAPTER THIRTEEN

River walked off. He watched the river while he collected drift-wood, carrying the branches back to where Huia huddled, exhausted, her cheek on the sun-warmed rock.

Taking the kaikōmako, māhoe and puku tawai from his pikau, he worked swiftly to ignite the beech fungus, placing it carefully among his pile of twigs and small branches. Huia slid down the boulders and sat staring at the fire. "What are we going to do?" she sighed.

"Nothing today."

Huia reached into River's pikau, took out the ureure and

broke it in two. When River had finished he reached down to pick up the hinaki. "I reckon we should try some bait this time."

Huia looked up at him.

"Like worms," River said.

Huia thought for a few seconds. "I could make a wee kete to put them in."

"Yeah, good. I'll go get them." River climbed up the boulders and into the forest.

Huia walked gingerly across the river stones to a clump of harakeke. With a broken rock she hacked off a blade of flax.

She sat, bent over her weaving, feeling the warmth of the fire. River returned. Eight earthworms wriggled in his dirty hands. He shoved them in the little kete Huia held up to him. With the last strip of flax Huia wove it closed, tying it to the inside of the hinaki. River walked across a shoal of stones and set the trap in a backwater.

Amongst the rocks he found a clutch of boulders to shelter them from the wind sweeping down the river. River dragged leafy branches from the forest to make a roof on their rock hut. He lay bracken on the shingle for their bed and fetched fern fronds to use as blankets.

River looked across to the eel trap. "Hey, it's moving!" He ran stumbling across the shoal of stones and jumped into the water, grasping the hinaki by its mouth. Water gushed out as he lifted it. A tuna thrashed inside.

"Gotcha!"

River struggled to untie the jerking trap from the branch. Grinning, he carried it back to Huia with the eel banging against the sides. "Hey, Huia, take a look at this!"

"Ho . . . is that what the shouting was about?" She peered into the trap. "Get it out, cuz. Whack it on the head."

River tipped the eel onto the ground. It slithered among the rocks. He grabbed a long stick and tried to jab the twisting eel through the gills. Huia dropped a rock on its head.

River laughed. "That's done it." They watched the eel's twitching body, grinning at one another.

"I'll go gut it." River shoved his fingers into the eel's gills and carried it to the stream. He scrubbed its skin with handfuls of tiny stones to wash off the slime. River smashed a rock, choosing a sharp edge to saw the eel open. It ripped at the skin.

"Useless . . . " He whacked the back of the rock with another. A sharp fragment sheared off. "Yeah. Way better."

Namu crawled into his ears and hung around his eyes. He slapped them with stinking hands, scooped out the guts and dropped them on the rocks. He rinsed the tuna before carrying it back to their fire.

A smile lit Huia's face. "What do you reckon to a boil up?" she asked.

"How're we going to do that?"

"Get us a nīkau branch. A dead one on the ground. One of those ones with a bowl at the end. You know, like for sliding down hills."

River found a damp grove of kiekie and nīkau where a tiny stream trickled into the river. He broke ureure from the kiekie and hungrily bit into its flesh. Grabbing a nīkau bowl from amongst the leaf litter, he filled it with ureure and walked back towards the smoke rising from their fire. Huia hadn't moved from it since they'd arrived at the river.

River stopped and looked at the sun sparkling on the swift water tumbling around boulders and rocks. Tomorrow he'd look for a calm place for them to cross. Huia's voice dragged him from his thoughts.

"Ka pai," she called.

"These too," he shouted back, walking over to her and dumping the ureure in her lap.

"Tumeke. Hey, get some water in the nīkau."

River looked at her. "Don't they ever say please in your part of the world?" Huia's face flushed, and she looked away.

Walking back across the stones, River balanced the nīkau bowl in his hands to keep the water from slopping over the side, stopping to rest halfway. He put in down next to Huia, then knelt and hacked at the eel with his rock knife.

"Get those two rocks I put in the fire," Huia said. "Drop them in the nīkau . . . please." River lifted the first one between two sticks. "Don't splash me, e cuz . . . chuck the tuna in."

They sat watching the steam rise from their nīkau pot as they waited for the eel to cook. River moaned. "When's it gonna be ready?"

"Won't be long. It'll turn white. You'll see."

River watched the eel. Saliva ran down his throat. "That's it . . . I'm in." He speared a piece.

"Hey, wait for me, e." They jabbed the rough chunks, spitting out the fine bones as they chewed, neither of them slowing until the eel was gone.

River wiped his mouth. "Good eh . . . just need the chips to go with it."

"Tumeke a-as." Huia sat back with a smile.

The cold came with the dusk. River dragged a driftwood log to the fire to smoulder through the night. Hugging Tau's Swanndri tight around her, Huia clambered slowly over the boulders to their rock shelter.

River checked the hinaki, tugging at the straps, tying the knots again, pushing the trap beneath the water. He crawled between the boulder walls of their hut and lay down next to Huia, covering himself with the scratchy ponga. "What are the namu like?"

"Bad."

River pulled his hood around his face, trying to shut out the hovering sandflies and jammed his eyes shut.

CHAPTER FOURTEEN

River woke in a stream of water. Rain poured through the fern roof. The river roared beside them, hurtling, rushing, smashing rock against rock.

"Huia! Wake up! We gotta get outa here!"

He shook Huia's shoulder. "Hey, wake up! The river's flooding!" Huia murmured, grumbling in her sleep. "Hurry! Get up, cuz!"

In the darkness, they stumbled over the rocks. "Ow!" Huia winced, clutching her ribs. Water swirled around their ankles freezing their feet. The boulders loomed over them. River placed his hand on the cold wet rock.

"We'll have to feel our way up," he said, putting his hand out for Huia to grab.

They slithered like crabs up the slippery boulders. Their hands, stiff with the cold, barely grasped the edges and nooks. Rain drenched their backs. Behind them, the river thundered, booming as logs smashed into rocks, shaking the ground under their feet.

"Here's the trees," River shouted. He strained to pull Huia up and helped her clamber beneath the dripping branches. Rain trickled down River's neck. He stepped back against the trunk of a tall beech. "Come back here out of the rain." Huia moved beside him. Her shivering reached through his hoodie and he felt the chill of her wet body. They stood like that for some time before sliding down to sit huddled together beneath the branches, their backs against the rough bark, sharing their meagre warmth. River felt Huia's head drop on his shoulder. He heard the heaviness of her breathing.

Beyond their tree, the rain lashed. The river deafened their world. River waited for the dawn, waited to see what the morning light would bring. He sighed. That was the hinaki gone for sure. And the fire. Exhaustion overcame him and he slept.

The birds began their songs for the new day. The rain had stopped. Stiff and sore, they stretched and groaned. "We sound like the kaumatua, eh?" said Huia. "Getting up from the mattresses."

"You tell me," River said. Huia looked at him. He stamped the ground to warm his cold damp body. The forest dripped. But through the canopy, Huia spied a patch of blue sky.

They stood shivering on the bank of boulders, staring at the swollen, dirty river rushing and tumbling where their fire and shelter had been. Water now spread from below their feet to the forest on the other side. Gone was the shingle, the shoals of small stones, the trickling rivulets. Logs and broken branches sailed by, bouncing down rapids and swinging wildly around boulders.

They found a place to sit among the boulders on the river bank, where the morning sun reached them but not the wind. Huia reached into the pikau. She handed a ureure to River, keeping another for herself. They leaned against each other, their clothes wet and their faces blue. With chattering teeth, they bit into the fruit.

River scavenged dry twigs and broken branches tucked in deep amongst the higher boulders. In the shelter of the rock, he built a small fire. They huddled over its heat to still their shivering. A bright sun rose in the sky. Its warmth touched their faces and dried their clothes.

"You know my mate, Dylan," River said. "He told me people reckon moose live in these forests."

"Moose? As if." Huia laughed. "And how would you kill a moose, cuz . . . if we ever ran across one?"

He grinned. "I'd find a way, don't you worry." He stood up.

"What's the river looking like?" Huia asked. River heard the tremor in her voice.

"Going down. Take all day, I reckon."

By late afternoon the river had dropped. River and Huia walked along on the boulders to a place where the river ran wide and shallow. In the middle, the current flowed and the water deepened. Huia stared at it for a long time.

"Cross in the morning, eh River? It'll be better then." He

saw her looking at him, willing him to say yes. "We can make a shelter in the boulders and sleep by our fire."

They headed back, gathering branches for their roof and dry wood for their fire. "I keep thinking about Dad . . . wondering what happened to him." Huia sighed. "I don't know what to think . . . what if he got washed up on the shore somewhere else?" River said nothing. "River . . . ?" He shrugged. What could he say?

They picked their way over the stones in silence. River picked up a long thin branch. "Looks like a spear, eh?" He fingered a sharp jagged end that tapered to a point. River felt the edge of the stone in his pocket. The one he'd used on the eel. He rested the pointy end of his spear on a boulder.

"Hold this, Huia? See if I can sharpen it."

She held the spear tight to the boulder as he gripped his stone knife in both hands and scraped at the wood. His arms ached but slowly the spear narrowed to a long point. "That might do it." River ran his thumb over the end. "I'll give it a go."

Huia laughed. "Bring us back a moose, cuz,"

"Ha. I might just do that."

River walked across the boulders and into the dripping forest. Wet leaves brushed his hoodie as he crept through the branches. Moss and mud squelched with each footstep. He looked back at the river and sniffed the air to smell smoke from their fire as he moved deeper into the forest and away from Huia. River looked for signs of movement among the saplings and bushes. He listened for sounds of rustling in the fern.

As he pushed past new fronds of bracken he saw a bird's claw print pressed into the mud. Big, like a hen's. River crouched down and looked at it closely. Fresh as. He grinned

His eyes scanned the debris of fallen branches and rotten logs between the beech trees. River trod softly, following the prints in the mud until they disappeared into the leafy humus. He hid among a clump of ponga and quietly waited. Listening.

The river hurtled and splashed, the birds in the trees called to one another. Come on, bird . . . I know you're in there somewhere. He sniffed the smoke from their fire and sighed. Come on . . . Something crunched the dead fern. River froze.

He raised his head to peek. A weka pecked among the fronds. Very slowly, he raised his spear and waited, poised and still. The weka came closer, head down, its strong beak poking and prodding the humus. Closer still. River held his breath. Suddenly the weka turned. He thrust his spear, driving it into the weka's chest. "Gotcha!"

"Hey, cuz!" River shouted as he hobbled across the stones, his spear in one hand, the weka in the other. "Don't think birds know about people in these parts."

CHAPTER FIFTEEN

In the morning River and Huia stood shivering at the widest part of the river, looking at the water flowing swiftly between them and the other side. A light mist hung over the water.

"It'll be shallowest here," River said.

Huia took a step. "Aue . . . this water's like ice."

The freezing water numbed their feet, making them stumble as they waded out. "Your ribs hurt?" River asked. Huia nodded. He watched Huia feeling with her hands for a way around the boulders, bracing herself against the water gushing either side. River waited, moving closer. "Here, use my spear for a walking stick." Huia shook her head.

The water deepened with each step. River's legs were numb to his thighs. Soon it would reach his hoodie. He looked at the water ahead of them in the main channel of the river.

"Riv . . . er!"

River spun around. Huia screamed. Water hurtled around her, knocking her off-balance. She slipped beneath the surface. "Huia!" River watched in disbelief as she swept downstream, her head disappearing and reappearing. She slammed against a boulder.

And then she was gone.

River leapt forward, fighting the current as he staggered across the channel, swearing angrily at the slippery rocks and rushing water. He hauled himself out to the dry stones and charged along the bank.

At the bend in the river, he froze. "No . . . o! Not rapids!" Ahead, the river swirled and frothed as it cascaded down rocks. White spray flew through the air. His heart pounded as he jumped from boulder to boulder looking desperately for Huia. He screamed her name again and again.

River stood at the head of the rapids, gasping for breath, his ears filled with the deafening crashing of water. In his mind he saw Huia washed down with the foam and spray, bashing into boulders, dragged under by logs. Pain ripped through him. He turned away angrily, swallowing against the lump in his throat. She couldn't be gone.

Go back, fool. Look properly.

He waded among the rocks, his eyes scanning the river for her red jacket, her curly black hair. He shouted again and held his breath.

A faint cry cut through the rushing water.

"Huia!" River scampered up a large boulder. "Huia? Huia! Where are you?"

"Help me, River."

"Hey, Huia, I'm here!" River hollered. "Where are you?" The river ran wide before him, white water coursed around boulders and the logs caught between them. And mid-stream, behind a large rock, a peek of red. He grinned and shouted, "I'm coming!"

Dumping his pikau and spear on the bank, River ran, slipping and sliding on the rocks under his feet. Striding out against the current towards the boulders, he slipped and fell beneath the freezing water. He dragged himself up. "Huia! I'm coming!"

"River?" Her voice was weak. And then she screamed at him. "Don't come around the front! Go to the back. Climb the boulder from the back!"

"Why?"

"Just do it, e!"

The water washed around his waist as River tried to grip the boulder. The current dragged at him, pulling him away from the rock. He clung on. His hand grabbed at a lump. His foot found a ledge and he hauled himself up to the top.

Huia looked up at him. Her eyes were wild with terror. Blood ran down her bruised face.

"I c-can't m-move. The w-water's too str-ong for me."

An eddy swirled around her, sucking her against the rock, pinning her to the boulder. "I can get you, cuz. Wait. I'll get you up." River lay on top of the boulder, his feet braced against ledges, his knees gripping the rock. He reached down and grabbed under her armpits.

"Find a ledge to stick your heel on."

"Got one. Hurry!"

"I'll count to three . . . then push up. Okay?"

"Hurry up!"

"One. Two. Three-e." Huia pushed down on her leg, her back and shoulders straining upwards. She found a cranny with her other heel and pushed up again. Her hands heaved against lumps in the rock. River clamped his knees hard to the boulder. Bit by bit, his arms screaming with pain, he pulled her up.

Huia clung onto the top. She looked at River, her eyes wide and staring. "I thought . . . I thought . . . I was a goner." River lay panting beside her. He didn't say a word.

River helped Huia down the back of the rock. He kept his body against the current while he guided her to the shore. They clambered out of the water and over the rocks to a pile of boulders and logs. Sheltered from the wind funnelling down the river valley they huddled together, drenched and shivering.

"Ow, my h-head." Huia felt the sticky blood in her hair. "My body took the meanest bash."

"You're alive." River smiled at her.

"Yeah, I'm alive." Huia smiled back.

"Gimme a look at your meanest bash." River looked at the patch of congealed blood matting her hair. "I'll need to wash the blood off to see it properly."

"Leave it for now, eh?" said Huia. "The bleeding might start up again."

River scrambled up the bank to gather driftwood for their fire. The wind froze his wet body. His hands shook as he took his sticks and puku tawai from his pikau. He rubbed the kaikōmako along the groove in the māhoe. Huia fought to hold it steady, wincing with each thrust. When a small curl of smoke smouldered in the wood dust, he placed the dried fungus on the tiny flame and waited for it to flare before dropping it gently into his pile of twigs.

They moved closer, warming their hands and their faces as River built up the fire, feeling the heat reach into their bodies.

"Half of me sh-shivers from the c-cold and half shiv-ers from sh-shock," Huia said. "I th-thought I was g-going to d-die, River."

River looked into the fire, remembering how he'd felt when he thought she'd gone.

CHAPTER SIXTEEN

They rested, letting the fire dry their clothes, chewing on the shoots from a mountain cabbage tree. River filled the base of one of its broad leaves with water and placed a hot rock in it. "A hot water cuppa coming up." He turned to Huia. "You dry yet?"

She nodded. "Let's move on. Away from this river. It spooks me."

River stopped poking the fire and turned to her. "But . . . you took a hammering."

"I don't care . . . Even if we only get a little way, we can leave this place behind us."

He looked at her closely and saw she was serious. He nodded. "Okay." River turned to watch the water sweeping around the rocky bluff. "Remember what we saw?" he said. "From up on the ridge? If we walk downstream we'll meet the river valley coming from the east."

"Ae, that's right. Come on. Let's go find it."

They picked their way along the boulders. On the river bank slender toetoe drooped, bobbing in the breeze, their white flower-heads ragged and spent. Huia stopped and unfurled a stem. She gave it to River. "Chew that."

"Hey, it's like that sugar cane. You ever had that?" Huia shook her head. "A hippy has it at the market in Westport. It's yum. Take some with us." He walked on. "You know, if we ever get back . . . "

"When we get back, River," Huia interrupted.

"Yeah. When we get back . . . " He turned to Huia, laughing. "I could have a stall at the Hokitika Wild Foods Festival."

"What? You think you're an expert now, cuz?"

He flicked his eyebrows.

Huia grinned. "You're a joke, River."

They came around the bend in the river. Huia stopped. She stared at the pounding rapids. At the spray hurling high in the air. Her legs shook. "I could have . . . "

"Come on," River said. "It never happened. Don't look."

They left the boulders and wove through the trees and the ferns with the river rushing beside them. They heard the rumble before they saw the deep swirling pool where the two rivers met for their journey to the coast. But River and Huia turned away, turned eastward, climbing gently with their new river. It spread in shallow braids crisscrossing the shingle, making it easy for them to ford.

Still they travelled slowly, without energy. Huia ached with each step. As they moved further up the valley the forest on both sides loomed closer and grew darker. The river narrowed and deepened. River stumbled with tiredness. "Stop, eh?"

River shrugged off his pikau and slumped to the rocks. Huia sat down beside him. "Enough for today?" he asked. She nodded. They sat in silence while they rested.

Eventually, River pushed himself up. "Sitting around's not gonna get us any kai." With no hinaki for eels, River tied a lure of small bushy branches in the slow water of a side-stream. While Huia built a fire on the shingle he propped long leafy branches of beech against the dirt bank nearby, with room for them to crawl beneath for the night.

Later, River walked slowly over the stones to his branches in the stream. Dark green kōura clung to their hiding places among the dense leaves. He grinned broadly. "Hey . . . at last," he called out. "At last I get to eat these fullas."

River knocked each one into steaming water in a nīkau bowl. He and Huia watched as the kōura turned orange. "Hope these are as good as you say, cuz." He flicked one from the water and broke open its hot shells. River sucked out the steaming white flesh. "Yeah," he grinned. "They are."

"Give us one, cuz. Don't hog them, e." River flicked a kōura to Huia. She smiled tiredly. "These gonna be on your menu?"

River laughed and flicked another kōura onto the rocks by Huia. He broke open another one for himself. "How's the head?"

"Still got a headache." Huia fingered the knotted mass of hair and dried blood. "And an egg, by the feel of it."

"You want me to look at it after?"

"Ae. That'd be good."

They walked down to the stream. River gently washed the blood from her hair. He parted her curls to peer at her scalp. "S'not too bad. It's not deep. More like a rough graze that's ripped your skin a bit. Concrete for brains, eh?"

"Yeah, tough as old boots. That's me."

"Mmmm . . . I don't know abou . . . " Huia punched his arm.

When the sun left their valley they crawled inside their lean-to. They lay shivering on fern, back to back, each thankful for the warmth of the other.

The next morning, the sky was clear and blue. The sun warmed the tops of the mountains but in their shaded valley, Huia and River stumbled around the frosty rocks, blowing on their hands and shaking their fingers. River grimaced as hunger pangs racked his body. "Better be more kōura this morning . . . "

He dragged the branches from the stream, chucking them down on the rocks and shouting to Huia. "Nothing. Not one."

She pulled a face, sighing. "I'm so starving. All we've got is toetoe."

River stomped over the rocks. Huia handed him half the toetoe shoots. He sighed. They stood side by side, gazing up at the tops as they chewed.

"Look at that sun, River. How long will it take us to get up there?"

"Forever."

River slung the pikau on his back, taking up his spear in one hand, the nīkau bowl in the other. Huia picked up a branch for a walking stick. "Hey, River. Who's the kuia now, eh?"

"Nan number two," he smiled. "How's your egg today?"

"Going down. My headache's not so bad. Not like yesterday."

Huia led, her tokotoko taking the strain from her sore ribs, her aches and her bruises. She followed the tumbling stream through the tall, brooding trees. Their bodies warmed as they climbed. River looked to the head of the valley where a spur climbed to the tops. So far away. He stopped. "I'm gutless today."

"We haven't eaten. That's why." Huia waited for him to catch his breath. "We have to keep going, River. We freeze when we stop."

Huia lumbered behind River as he picked his way over the rocks by the stream. They clambered through the trees, digging their sticks into the humus, battling for each step to haul themselves up the steep mountainside.

River leaned against a tree-trunk. Huia waited behind him. "I've forgotten what it's even like to have energy," he said.

"Me too."

He turned to Huia, puffing. "You know . . . I came third . . . in the 1500 metres at school . . . Now I'd have to walk the 100."

"I'd have to crawl it," Huia grunted. "Least your ribs don't feel like they're stabbing you. Come on, cuz, we've gotta keep moving."

River didn't reply. He dug his spear into the bank and carried on. It hurt to breathe in the forest's freezing air. He pulled his hoodie up in front of his mouth, letting the air mingle with his body heat. He looked up at the blue, blue sky and the sharp lines of the rocky tops in the clear mountain air, the bright sunlight vivid against the dark green of their valley. He sighed. It'd take days to get there at this rate.

River turned, looking down at Huia, watching her struggle and knew they couldn't keep going like this. If they didn't eat they'd never make it.

CHAPTER SEVENTEEN

They came to a place near the stream on the edge of the forest and lay among the rocks, too exhausted to look for food, letting the midday sun seep into their tired bodies.

Eventually, hunger drove River to get up. He made a fire and left Huia sleeping beside it. Taking his spear, he walked softly through the forest. He heard the stream tripping down the mountain and the wind in the trees, heard the birdsong and scuttling among the ferns. As River listened to the life of forest he began to feel part of it.

Wings flapped above him and he looked up. To the round white belly of a kereru. He smiled as he watched the bird flying from tree to tree, perching on branches and waddling among the leaves.

"Gotcha," he said softly to himself. He grabbed some miro berries and stuffed them in his pocket. Grasping the branch of a tōtara, River pulled his body up and climbed higher into the tree. He found a place to line the berries along a branch. Miro berries in a tōtara tree, he chuckled. That kereru won't believe its luck. River hid, crouching behind the tōtara's flaky trunk. He waited, listening for the swishing beat of the kereru's wings. His calves ached.

River thought of his wild beach near Fox River and his mother alone in their cottage. He wished she knew he was still alive. That he was trying to get home.

Woosh. Woosh.

River raised his spear as he watched the wood pigeon swoop in. Its feet gripped the branch. Eyes still, the bird turned its head from side to side. River held his breath. The kereru blundered along the branch and dipped its beak to the first berry. And the next. River inched his arm back.

Two flaps and the bird was gone.

"What?" He pulled himself up on the trunk as he watched the kereru fly away through the trees. River hurled his spear to the ground. He dropped from a branch and crashed through the forest to the fire.

Huia looked up at his face. "What's with you?"

River grunted. "Nothing." He looked at the rocks heating the water in the nīkau bowl beside the fire. "What you making?"

"Doughboys." She laughed at his puzzled face. "See . . . I smash up these hīnau berries. Get rid of the skins and stones . . . and I'm left with this doughy stuff. Watch."

She scooped up the flesh of the hinau, shaped it into a sticky ball with her hands and placed it in the steaming water. Huia hooked one out with a stick for him to try.

"These are gross."

"Yeah, they are, eh? I know . . . I think the dough's meant to be cooked in a hangi first."

"Well, that's not gonna happen."

"Nah . . . but you can still eat them, cuz. It's okay to eat hinau."

River grimaced and gulped as he forced another one down. It was food and it was hot. He sat down on a large log, feeling its damp seep through his jeans, holding his hands to the fire.

"I couldn't get a bird," he said, rubbing his arms. Huia glanced at him, but said nothing, handing over more doughboys. River looked down at his hands. They'd turned skinny. His wrist bones stuck out. He'd be a walking skeleton if they didn't get over the mountains soon. He dug around on the rotten log, peeling off handfuls of slushy wood, chucking it to the ground.

River built up the fire to warm them. He fiddled with the log, his fingers poking the holes and tunnels of the wet wood. Something slid against his fingertip and he snatched his hand back.

"Yuck."

"What?"

"There's something . . . "

They grinned at each other. "Huhu bugs." River pulled away the wood and he and Huia grabbed at the fat white grubs.

"You eaten them before?" Huia asked him. River shook his head. She held a huhu by its head, dropping the wriggling body into her open mouth. "Mmm . . . yum. Peanut butter."

River screwed up his face, shuddering as the insect moved on his tongue, but when he bit it, he smiled. "Yeah. You're right. Not bad." They dug out more, eating them alive and then trying them cooked in the water. "We should take some with us."

"Ae. Berries too," Huia said. "There'll be nothing to eat on the tops. 'Less you can spear us one of those moose."

"Mmm . . . imagine it though. Roast venison. Now that's what I call a feed. Beats berries hands down."

"Yeah, I could make a fancy berry sauce to go with it. Like you see on those cooking shows," Huia laughed.

Always staying close enough to smell the fire, they wandered through the forest, River listening for the rustling of a weka in the fern, Huia with her eyes on the plants. They ripped shoots from the fat toi, the mountain cabbage tree, picked kareao and miro berries. Huia gathered more of the fleshy fruit of the hīnau and orange berries from the kakaha.

That evening they slept in beds of bracken and fern by the fire, snuggled under the scratchy fronds with only their noses and mouths in the freezing night air. River had dragged an old log to the fire and it smouldered hour after hour.

By the morning their bedding was wet with dew. They scrambled up. Huia stamped her feet, hugging Tau's Swanndri tightly around her. River fed the embers and heated the rocks to warm their water. They chewed on mountain cabbage tree shoots and drank kawakawa tea, trying to stave off their aching hunger, trying to get warmth into their bodies.

Huia looked at River. "Let's get going eh? I can't even feel my toes they're so cold."

They clambered up through the forest. River jammed his left hand deep in his hoodie pocket, but his right hand stung with cold as he grasped his tokotoko. His breath hung like white puffs in the early morning light.

As they climbed higher the forest changed. The beech no longer stood tall and proud but grew twisted and gnarled in its relentless battle against the winds for a foothold on the mountain tops. River and Huia pushed through the stringy lichen swinging from the dark trees. Huia caught her first glimpse of tussock through the trees. Clumps of flax marked the edge of the forest.

"Try this, River." With frozen hands, she dug out sticky gum at the base of the long leaves of harakeke. She scraped the gum off her fingers with her teeth. River watched her.

"You don't eat it. You just chew it. Try some, e."

River dug a finger in. "Yeah, not bad," he grinned. "I'd need to add a flavour though. Got any ideas?"

"You still going on about your stall?"

"Yeah . . . I'm on a winner. Think of a name for my stall, cuz."

"River's Rotten . . . mmm . . . I'll have to think of the rest."

River laughed. "Hey, how's the feet?"

"Numb. Numb to everything."

"Same here."

As they stepped past the harakeke and out of the forest the wind caught them. Huia pulled her jacket collar tight around her neck. Digging her tokotoko into the mud she hauled herself, step by step, to the mountain-tops. The wind whipped away their words and they climbed through the waving tussock in silence.

CHAPTER EIGHTEEN

They stood at the summit resting on their tokotoko. The cold wind made their eyes water, then blew their tears away. In the distance rose Tākitimu. A powdering of snow dusted its grey peaks.

"Our wa-ka." River chattered. His teeth ached with the cold. "We an-y clos-er, you rec-kon?"

Huia pulled up Tau's Swanndri to cover her head. "Ae. We are." They stood together, their eyes on their turangawaewae. Their way home.

River drew his hood tight around his face until just his eyes and red nose were showing. Buffeted by the winds, he pointed out their route along a ridge to a rocky peak. From there another ridge veered towards a higher mountain in the east.

A sudden gust sent them scrambling for cover down the sheltered side of the peak. They lay face down on the scree. River looked up. Except for scurrying white clouds the sky was clear. "We need to keep moving. While the weather's good."

They dropped from the peak, sliding down the scree to the ridge. Using their tokotoko to steady themselves against the icy winds, they trudged along the backbone of the mountains.

River's feet dragged. Before him stood Tākitimu. He walked towards it unable to think. About the strength he didn't have or the hunger with him always. Not thinking about the pain in his fingers and toes or the stinging cold of his face. He looked only at where his next step would go.

Huia stopped suddenly. "We're for it now, cuz."

River looked up. His eyes widened. A mass of dirty cloud barrelled straight towards them. He pushed Huia's shoulder. "Go . . . hurry!"

They staggered along the tops, feeling the cold arrive and

drive into them. River saw the first flutter of snow on Huia's curls and torn Swanndri. Snowflakes blew in his face. "Let me go in front. Stick close to me."

Shivering, he pushed into the snowstorm, moving slowly to let Huia shelter behind him, hearing her ragged breathing and snuffling nose. River peered through the swirling snow at a large outcrop of rock further along the ridge. He pointed at it. Huia nodded.

Heads down, they fought the wind along the ridge until the rocks suddenly appeared before them. River scurried around, searching for an overhang, a cave, anything to give them shelter. He pulled Huia into a gap and they lay, squashed together, shivering as the snow settled on the rocks above.

The deepening snow muffled the wind. A ledge caught the snow, leaving a clear space where cold air entered. River groaned. There was nothing they could do but stay where they lay.

During the afternoon they turned and twisted, trying to escape the wet seeping through their clothing. Stones bit into their bodies. The light changed and River knew it would soon be night. He lay listening to the howling wind, heard Huia's breathing deepen as she drifted off to sleep.

He slept for a snatch of time, waking with a violent shiver. Huia cuddled into him in her sleep and he jumped at her coldness. River drew her close to stop her shivering. Like him, she had grown so thin.

Each time River woke during the night, he heard the menace in the wind. He lay awake, sick with fear, his thoughts racing. How long could they last like this? Cold as. Never having enough to eat.

In the light of dawn, River watched the flying snowflakes through the gap, listening to the wind racing along the ridge. Huia slept fitfully beside him. She opened her eyes and clasped her shivering body. "I'm so, so cold."

"It's snowing again."

"I have to get moving, River. I'll turn to ice if I don't."

"Huia, listen to the wind . . . "

"I bet it's always windy up on the tops. I'm not lying here

'til I shiver to death. I have to get back. I have to tell Mum about Dad."

River had no answer to that.

They ate the last of their huhu grubs and dug out handfuls of snow to melt in their mouths. Huia's numb hands fumbled as she wriggled to tuck in her jersey and pull down her jacket.

"You ready?" River asked. She nodded. Lying on his stomach he pushed snow out of their tunnel. He crawled out and jumped up.

"Hurry, Huia!"

River stamped the ground, shoving his stinging hands under his armpits. Huia pushed his pikau and spear out of the tunnel, followed by her tokotoko. As her head emerged the wind picked up her curls. She grabbed them to her head.

"It's worse out here, River. Way worse."

"You're the one who wanted to go on. Hurry up." River tightened his hood and pulled his sleeves down. "Go in front of me."

He kept close to Huia, shielding her from the cold, cold wind on his back as they mushed through the ankle-deep snow.

Its iciness seeped into their shoes, stinging their toes as they trudged along the ridge towards its peak now thick with snow. The wind froze their wet clothing and turned their faces blue. It drove them on, desperate to escape the cold.

They dug their tokotoko into the snow and scree as they climbed the peak before them. River's breath rasped his throat. At the summit the wind hurled at them, blinding their eyes with tears. They squinted at what lay ahead. Another ridge. And beyond, in the distance, Tākitimu.

"It's so far away," Huia whispered. River looked at Huia's drawn face and turned away. There was nothing he could change. They had to keep going. They sloshed down off the peak, snow filling their shoes and saturating the bottoms of their pants. River noticed Huia looking down at her trackies. They were wet to her knees.

They tramped the ridge, their shuddering bodies no match for the bullying wind. It pushed them around and stole their warmth. Huia grabbed at the Swanndri to keep it covering her head. River crashed into her. Huia jabbed the snow with her tokotoko staggering to stay upright. She turned to River. He stared speechless at her ashen face, her wild eyes.

"You okay?" he whispered.

Huia turned away without answering. River kept close behind as her steps became shorter and slower. He no longer felt his toes or his fingers.

River looked ahead. Ridge after ridge, peak after peak, and he knew that in the end, the cold would beat them. The wind and the wet would win.

CHAPTER NINETEEN

Their calves ached as they climbed the ridge towards the eastern peak. Their breath became ragged. They stopped often, dragging air into their lungs. Huia's shivering never stopped. It seemed to River like she climbed in a dream. Her tokotoko first, then her right foot, then her left, hauling herself up through the snow to the peak.

He saw Huia reach the summit. Her head dropped and her shoulders began to shake. River struggled to get to her. "What's up, cuz?"

Huia tottered at the edge of a jagged rock-face. One step and she'd be gone. River grabbed the back of her jacket and pulled her to him. She stared at the precipice falling away at their feet. "I can't go on . . ."

He lifted her head. "Look. Tākitimu. Our waka. Our tupuna. They're walking with us, remember." Silently, she nodded.

He led Huia down off the peak, his arm around her shoulders, keeping her shivering body close to his side. She felt so cold. Beyond talking, beyond caring. "Come on . . . we'll get off the tops." River looked for a way down the barren stones and waving tussock.

The icy wind lifted their damp clothes and froze their wet skin as they slid down the loose scree through the skittering snow. River stumbled to the ground, dragging Huia with him. "Sorry, cuz." He pulled her up and brushed the snow from her clothes. "You all right?" Huia barely nodded. River shook the snow from his dreads. "Come on, it'll be better down . . . " He stopped talking. Huia looked at his staring eyes, his open mouth.

"What . . . what? What is it?"

"Look . . ."

She followed his gaze to a small pile of rocks. Like a cone.

Larger rocks had been placed at the bottom with smaller rocks on top.

"People," she whispered.

"Yeah . . . people . . . someone's made that."

They looked at each other in disbelief, slowly smiling. Tears trickled down Huia's cheeks.

"We're gonna make it. We're going home."

River's eyes shone. He grinned at her. Head back, his fists clenched at his sides, he shouted at the sky. "Yes!" He laughed out loud. "Kia ora to you, Tākitimu."

Huia laughed too. "You're getting there, cuz." She saw the next cairn further down the slope. "Hey, look, River. Who makes them?" Huia asked.

He turned. "Hunters and trampers. To show the way on the tops."

Smiling and laughing, shaking their heads, they plodded down through the tussock towards the next cairn. River pointed to an orange triangle nailed to a mountain beech down at the edge of the forest. "It's the beginning of a track."

Huia grinned at him. "We're safe. We are, eh? Aren't we?" River flicked his eyebrows, smiling.

At the triangle marker, the forest folded around them and the relentless wind was left outside.

Looking for glimpses of orange, they followed the winding track through the gnarled trees, happy to go where it led, knowing each step took them closer to somewhere and wherever that was, it was closer to home.

They sidled through the mountain beech, their legs weary, their feet numb.

As the trees became taller and straighter River knew they were dropping down, away from the tops and deeper into the forest with its damp dark valleys.

The track twisted and turned through the thick forest, the dark greens and browns broken only by the orange triangle markers.

Huia looked ahead, her eyes taken by a broad flash of bright orange among the trees. She frowned. "What's that?"

River looked up. A grin split his face.

"What?" she said.

He dragged himself into a run leaving her behind. "You'll see," he called over his shoulder.

"Come back, you." Huia looked at River disappearing along the track. His laughter floated back through the trees. "What are you doing, e?" She stomped after him.

Without warning, Huia stepped into a clearing. A small orange hut sat alone in the grass. River sat on the porch, grinning at her, the door open behind him.

"There's food," he called.

Huia stumbled across to the hut. "Hey?"

"Baked beans and stuff."

"Don't make it up, River."

"Nah, true."

"Let me see . . . "

Huia stood in the doorway and her whole face smiled. Bunks, a table and stools. A small wood burner with a blackened billy and an old frying pan. A tin of baked beans, flour, a packet of rice risotto sat on a shelf.

"Tell me I'm not dreaming, cuz."

He grinned back at her. "You wanna start with baked beans?"

"Yes, anything," she said, as she collapsed on a bunk. She

stretched out and lay without moving, the hard mattress **soft** to her aching body.

River whacked the can with an axe. Tomato sauce ran down his hand. He licked it clean. "Yum." He tipped the beans into a billy.

Huia struggled up to sit side by side with River. Scooping the tangy beans into their mouths, laughing and gobbling until the last bean was gone. Huia wiped her finger around the sauce on the top of the billy. "I can't believe it . . . I'm full already."

"Me too," said River. "Our stomachs must've shrunk to nothing. I'll make us some soup, eh?"

Still grinning, River grabbed kindling and branches from the woodpile on the porch. A squashed box of matches sat on the table, next to the stub of a candle. Huia watched him light a fire in the wood burner and waited for its heat to reach out to her.

He heated water in the billy, scraping and mixing in any leftover sauce.

Soon the smell of warming tomato sauce filled the hut. Taking turns, they gulped down the weak soup.

Sighing, Huia lay back down on the closest bunk. River filled the burner with chunks of wood and slid onto another mattress. With the warmth of the fire on his face, his eyes slipped shut.

He woke with a start and Huia snored again. River grinned. Quietly, he swung his legs off the bunk and placed more wood in the firebox. He stood warming his back, drying off his hoodie, his damp jeans. He rubbed his hands up and down his arms. Huia snorted. She's out to it, he chuckled. River looked at her sleeping and felt a stab of sadness.

CHAPTER TWENTY

That night Huia made a kind of Maori bread, mixing flour into a dough with water, patting out hunks to fry in the pan.

"Fried bread. I never would have thought . . . not in a million years . . . we'd be eating fried bread tonight. After last night, eh?" River said, wiping his mouth.

"Yeah, last night huhu grubs in an igloo," Huia laughed. "And tonight fried bread in a nice warm hut."

They washed the bread down with manuka tea. The warmth of the food settled inside them. Sharing the candle, they pored over remnants of hunting magazines until they were overcome

with tiredness. River loaded the wood burner with logs and closed down the damper.

In the night the cold woke him and he poked more wood on the embers. Too cold to sleep he lay on his bunk, waiting for the fire's warmth, thoughts playing through his mind. Behind the long drop, he'd seen where the track continued on. To another DOC hut, he felt sure. And maybe another one after that. But eventually the track would end at a road and a road would lead to farmhouses, people and phones.

He smiled, thinking of the surprise in his mother's voice when he rang. She mightn't believe it at first. He thought of their homecoming at Riverton. The whanau. Their joy at seeing Huia and River alive . . . their sadness at losing Tau. Wanting to know what happened. Putting things right.

And after that. He and Mum driving back up to the West Coast. Saying goodbye to Huia. And then it came again, that same dragging feeling. They'd been through so much together. The two of them.

Even with the morning sunshine coming through the window Huia slept on and on. River made himself tea and fried bread. He filled the billy with water to heat **and grabbing** a scrap of soap by the tank stand went behind the hut for **a** wash. He washed his hair and his body, tipping the billy over his head to rinse off the soap. His skin came alive, clean and tingling in the morning sun.

The door to the hut scraped the floor as River pushed it open. Huia opened her eyes. "That was so good," he said. "I've had a wash. You should try it." She rubbed her eyes. "I'll make you some breakfast, eh Huia?" He patted out some leftover dough.

Even with breakfast inside her Huia didn't seem to feel like moving from the bunk.

"I feel so-o gutless," she said. "Like I've got nothing left to make my legs work."

"We don't have to go today," River said. "There's food here." He nodded at the packet of rice risotto. "Probably some in the next hut too."

"River . . . " Huia looked up at him. "What am I going to say about Dad, you know, when I see them? Mum and Nan."

He shrugged. "Whatever you say, you'll stop them

wondering, Huia. Wondering what happened. That must help. Big time."

Huia dozed throughout the morning. River found dry branches in the forest and dragged them back to the hut. He broke off the brittle ends for kindling and chopped the thick branches to stack in the wood bin. He saw Huia stagger off into the trees, billy in one hand, soap in the other. Heard her gasping as the water sloshed over her. He smiled to himself.

She stood before him, back in her dirty clothes. River looked at her crazy curls starting to escape the weight of the water.

"What are you staring at?" she said.

River shook his head, embarrassed. "Nothing," he mumbled, bringing the axe down on a fat branch.

"You want the risotto for lunch?" Huia asked.

"Yeah," he nodded, not looking at her. Huia went inside. Did it bother her? That soon she'd be in Riverton and he'd be back in Fox River. Away from each other. Getting on with their lives on their own.

The rice risotto was the best thing. Hot, savoury and filling. They struggled with the last mouthfuls but didn't stop. In the afternoon River lay around reading the torn magazines again while Huia slept.

He crept out of the hut. He sat in the quiet of the forest with his back against a tree trunk, thinking about all that had happened. Everything he'd learned. Knowing he needed to know more. What his tupuna knew. In his mind, he saw his father's marae, the whare tupuna waiting among the farmland near Huia's home and heard its silent karanga reach out to him.

River looked up to see Huia threading her way through the forest. She sat down next to him and leaned back against the tree trunk. They sat looking at the bright pockets of sunlit ferns and saplings among the shadows of the beech. "You know, River," she said, "I would never have made it without you."

He turned his head. "How d'ya mean? You were the one who knew everything. About what to eat. And catch. Making fire."

"Yeah, but you were the one who did it . . . who did the work . . . who took good care of me when my ribs were so sore. You were the one . . . always."

River didn't know what to say. He thought about what she'd said. He hadn't thought about it back then. He had just got on and done it. But it was true. River couldn't stop the smile filling his face.

Huia smiled back. "You know, you should come down more and stay with us," she said.

"Yeah." His eyes crinkled. "I will. I'd like that. Take me with you to the marae, eh."

"Course."

"I want to learn stuff . . . Dad mightn't be here but others are. They'll teach me, eh?"

"What do you think, cuz?" Huia laughed. "You try and shut Nan up. She won't let it go."

CHAPTER TWENTY-ONE

The next morning they stood outside the hut, River with his pikau on his back and Huia, her tokotoko in her hand. "I told you our tupuna are walking with us," she said.

"Ae. They are."

River pulled the door closed and together they set off down the track through the mist hanging in the trees. By mid-afternoon, they'd reached the next hut. Bright orange again, with walls of tin. A tin of stew and a can of peaches waited for them there. And a pile of old books.

The following day they tramped on, their legs weary, their

feet sore. The forest dripped with a light rain. All day they sloshed through puddles and sloppy mud. Drizzle seeped into their clothes and with it the cold. It was dusk before River spotted the next hut through the trees.

"At last . . ." sighed Huia.

"This one's big as. Look . . . it's even got a deck."

"I thought we'd never get here." Huia plonked herself down on the steps and pulled off her muddy trainers. "Kai and a fire. That's what I need." She turned when River opened the door. "Un . . . tidy."

"There's heaps of bunks." River looked around inside. "Must have more people using it." He grinned at Huia. "Hey, might be closer to a road."

"D'ya think, cuz?"

"Yeah. I do."

Huia smiled tiredly.

River turned. "So . . . what's for tea?"

They left the hut early in the morning. River led, his eyes on the muddy track. Before long he found what he was looking for. Boot marks. Lots of them.

"Look . . . it's a hut that's used heaps."

Huia grinned. "Maybe today, cuz . . . "

"Yeah . . . maybe . . . come on." They hurried their steps but River soon slowed. "Far, I'm puffed already."

"Ae, me too."

The track flattened as it wound closely through the tall, wet beech. Moss lined both sides of the path. Moss covered everything, the dripping tree trunks, the rotting logs they clambered over.

On and on they walked.

"How much further...?" said Huia. "Look at my shoes, will'ya? They couldn't be more muddy if . . . "

"Shhh..." River stopped. "What was that?"

A dog barked.

"Get in, Gus. Get in, I said."

River looked at Huia. They grinned tiredly at each other.

"Hey!" River shouted as they stumbled out of the forest and onto a dirt road.

A skinny young man crouched by an old ute, poking his rifle

behind the seat. "What ya barking at, Gus?" The dog barked again. "What is it, mate?"

"Us," called out River.

The hunter stood up. "What the …?" He wiped his black beanie over his face as they walked towards him. "Boy, you could each do with a couple of pies. What's going on? Where's your folks?"

River found he couldn't talk. He looked to Huia. "We were shipwrecked," she said.

"Eh? The sea's miles away. What are you talking about? It's on the other side of the . . . " He stopped. "You're not those . . . Not those kids who went down with the fishing trawler?"

They both nodded.

"Eh . . .? Where's your dad?" Huia looked at him and he saw the answer in her eyes.

"Right . . . " He took a breath. "I'm sorry, girl. Real sorry. That's real sad." He sighed. "Not good at all." He turned to River. "I better get you two home. Pronto. Some people are gonna be very happy to see you. Very happy. Where d'you kids live?"

"Riverton."

"Near Fox River."

"Riverton I can do. D'ya wanna call your families? Or . . . d'ya want to just get there?"

Huia and River looked at each other. "See them face to face." Huia turned to the young hunter. "I've got to tell them about Dad."

"Right." He looked at the ground. "Jump in, then." He threw his pack on the tray next to the kennel. "I'm Steve, by the way."

They squeezed themselves into the front seat. The ute bumped into potholes and over corrugations as they drove along the narrow road through the forest.

"You guys are looking pretty skinny on it. How long's it since you had a decent feed?"

"A long, long time," answered River.

Steve kept up the questions but their answers began to fall away. Huia sat quietly beside River as he looked out the window at the passing farmland and the cars whizzing by. It seemed so strange. He thought about his phone call home to

Denise and felt the excitement mount in the pit of his stomach. He put his arm around Huia and squeezed her shoulder. She gave him a little smile, then looked down at her hands.

Steve pulled into a petrol station and emerged with five steaming pies in his hands. He handed them two each. "Here you go. Like I said. Reckon you could each do with a couple of pies."

River shook his head, laughing. "Thanks, mate. I'll do my best." Huia smiled her thanks. "Oh, man," River said as he bit into it. "Mince and cheese." He managed to eat most of his second pie, but Huia handed hers to Steve.

They came to a small town. The main street was busy with camper-vans, tourists and locals. River and Huia stared at all the people.

"Tuatap," said Steve. "This is where I live."

"Tuatapere," said Huia.

"What?"

"It's Tuatapere. That's how you say it."

"Yeah. Right. Well, not too far to Riverton now."

River looked over at Huia but she stared straight ahead.

• • •

They drove along the coast. River looked out over **the blue sea.**
How long had it been since they had chugged through **those**
waves? Tau at the helm. Everything as it should be.

As the outskirts of Riverton came into view, Steve turned
to River. "Where to, mate?" As River gave directions, he felt
Huia stiffen beside him.

"It'll be all right," he whispered in her ear.

Steve drew up outside a wooden house. A straight concrete
footpath led through the hedge to the front door. "I'll wait
here in the ute."

Huia murmured her thanks and climbed out of the cab.
River shook Steve's hand. "You've been awesome. Thanks."

"It's nothing, mate. Glad I could help." He tipped his head
towards Huia standing on the pavement. "Good luck," he said
quietly.

CHAPTER TWENTY-TWO

Huia looked to River and they walked up the path towards the house. The front door flew open before they reached it. Cheryl came running down the steps wrapping her arms around Huia. Nan appeared at the doorway. Her hands flew to her face, "My mokos!" she cried. River stood there grinning, then leapt to embrace her. He felt the wetness of her cheeks as she pressed her face to his.

"Mum . . . " said Huia, holding herself back to look at her mother's face. "Dad . . . "

River saw the sorrow in Cheryl's eyes as she looked at Huia. "It's all right, Huia. I know. We kept hoping, hoping.

His fishing mates went up the coast, time after time, searching for you all. But in the end . . . I sensed he had gone. Nan felt it too." She hugged Huia to her. "Tangaroa's looking after him now."

"Did they find . . . anything, Mum?"

"No, babe, they didn't. They really didn't know where to look."

Eventually, Cheryl looked over at River. "We need to ring your mum. Now. But how did you . . . ?" River turned to look down the path. The ute had gone.

"My turn for a cuddle," said Nan. She clasped Huia tightly. "Feel that. Skin and bone. Come in and have a kai, my moko."

"What about one of your kawakawa teas, Nan?" River asked. Huia laughed. Her eyes sparkled as she looked at him.

"Eh?" said Nan.

"Nothing," River and Huia chorused.

"Sit down and tell us everything," said Cheryl, "but first . . . River . . . the phone's in the hallway."

River rang Denise. "Mum, it's River." There was silence. "Mum, it's River. I'm back. I'm in Riverton." He heard a sob.

"It's all right, Mum. I'm all right. Huia's all right. Tau's . . . Tau's dead, Mum."

". . ."Oh . . . son . . . " He heard her sob, heard her breathe. "River, is that really you?"

"Yes, Mum. It really is."

He felt her smile down the phone.

Denise arrived the next day.

She and River walked down to the wharf. He wished she wouldn't hold onto his arm. He looked around, then remembered it was a school day. No kids.

"I rang Hemi to tell him you were safe and well." River held his breath and waited for Denise to go on. "But I had to leave a message. He's away doing his two-week shift out on the oil rig."

"Where?"

"Off Western Australia. Way up from Perth somewhere." When River didn't reply, Denise carried on. "He came back to Riverton when he heard you were lost at sea."

River looked at Denise.

"He helped in the search but in the end, he had to go back
To finish his contract. He's got plans to bring back money for
a new trawler. He wants to fish out of Riverton. Take Tau's
place looking after the whanau."

River looked ahead, feeling his chest tighten. "How do you
know all this, Mum?"

"When you were missing he came up to see me."

"And . . . ?"

"We'll see, River, we'll see."

Cheryl was chopping up a pumpkin on the kitchen bench
when River and Denise returned to the house. "The others are
up at the marae. Why don't you go up and see them, River?"

"Yes, you go, River," said Denise. "I'll stay here with Cheryl
and give her a hand with dinner."

"Good idea," said Cheryl. "Give us a chance to have a nice
little korero. You know the way, don't you, tama?"

He flicked his eyebrows. As he walked out the door he
smiled to himself. Bet I know who they'll be talking about.

The marae was a little way out of town, away from the coast.

River stopped at the gateway. He gazed at the whare tupuna and whare kai sitting among the green of the surrounding paddocks and felt a calmness settle within him.

As River walked up the path he heard Nan and Huia's chattering coming from the whare tupuna and saw their shoes at the doorway. He peered inside. They sat on a side bench with their backs against the wall. Two brooms lay on the floor beside them.

"Haere mai, my moko," Nan called. "Come and join us. We tried to do some sweeping but this kotiro here is too tuckered out."

"It wasn't just me, Nan," Huia laughed.

River took off his shoes and walked over.

"E noho, moko, e noho," Nan said. He sat down next to her and leaned back. "You haven't been here for a long, long time, River," Nan paused and looked at him. "Do you remember anything about the whare tupuna?"

"Not really." River looked upwards, his eyes travelling the length of ridgepole.

"The whare tupuna represents the body of our ancestor,

River. Yours, Huia's and mine. That ridgepole there, te tahuhu, is the backbone, and the rafters, nga heke, the ribs." Nan turned to Huia, "Moko, I forgot to ask. Your ribs. What did the doc say yesterday?"

"She sent me for an X-ray, but yeah, all good. She said it was mending nicely."

"Ka pai, my moko."

River gazed at the large pole supporting the ridge. "What about that pole, Nan?"

"Ae, that's te pou tokomanawa. The link between Ranginui, the Sky Father, and Papatuanuku, the Earth Mother." Nan started to struggle up. "Time for our kai, I reckon. Enough korero for now. I'll tell you more next time, River. And you better be listening."

River grinned as he helped her to her feet.

The next day there were tears and hugs as the whanau stood beside Denise's car saying their goodbyes. River stood awkwardly before Huia.

She stepped forward wrapping her arms around him. "Don't

forget, you're coming down for the holidays. No changing your mind, cuz." She wiped her cheek.

River looked at her, smiling. "I won't."

"You bet you won't, moko," Nan said. "I'm going to need your muscle to do some clearing up at the marae. So go home and get eating." She squeezed his biceps. "Turn those pipi back into kutai."

EPILOGUE

"That was Cheryl on the phone. They're having a memorial service for Tau. It's the anniversary of his passing next month. I said we'd go down."

River looked up from his homework. "For sure."

Denise sat down at the table. "Can't believe it's nearly a year since I was down there."

"I've been down every holiday . . . just about."

Denise turned to River. "It's good you're getting to see more of your dad."

River flicked his eyebrows. "Yeah, he's all right. I like going out on the trawler."

Denise spoke quietly. "Give him a chance, River."

"I am. I will. But you know what they say in the cheese ad, Mum. Good things take time."

Denise laughed. She leaned over and hugged him to her. "You're hopeless."

River grinned at her. "Anyway. Guess he and I will be bringing in the kai moana for the memorial service."

"Maybe you should go down a few days earlier, then. I can't really leave the shop for too many days." Denise turned to him. "That bus trip is such a haul for you . . . "

River laughed. "There's no quick way to get to Riverton, Mum. I don't care. I like it down there. I like being with Huia and her mates. And up at the marae too."

Denise smiled. "That Nan works you, doesn't she?"

"I don't mind. She's nice as. She tells me heaps of stuff. She doesn't care how many questions I ask."

River and Huia walked along the road towards the marae. Huia carried photos of Tau in her kete for the memorial service.

"How was your day yesterday? With your dad," she asked.

"Yeah, good. He's all right, really. Once you get to know him."

River fell quiet. Yesterday had been great. Out on the waves. Hauling in the long lines and pulling up the craypots. They'd had some good laughs. River smiled as he thought about carrying the fish bins into the whare kai. The smiles and hugs that greeted them. It had felt good. Had felt real.

He turned to Huia, "What about you?"

"About Tau, do you mean?"

"Yeah."

"It's getting easier. But when you see things that remind you . . . " Huia looked ahead. "He'll always be with me, River."

"Yeah, he will."

She pulled a framed photo from the kete. "This one here's my favourite." River looked down at Tau's smiling face. Head back, laughing, his eyes alight. Just like that night in Tamatea Dusky Sound. Just as he would always remember him.

"Here comes your dad, River." River looked up to see Hemi coming down the road to meet them. His long loping strides, the same black curly hair as Huia. As he came closer River saw the concern in his eyes. Hemi stopped and waited for them.

"How are you this morning, Huia? Are you ready for this? The memorial service and everything."

Huia looked up at the man who looked so like her father and nodded.

"Remember, I'm here for you too." Smiling, he put his hand on River's shoulder. "Not just for this fulla."

• • •

EDIBLE NATIVE PLANTS

HĪNAU

Hīnau fruit look similar to a purple olive. Maori traditionally soaked the hīnau in water before pounding and sifting them to separate the flesh from the skin and stone. The flesh was mixed with water to make a dough which was steamed in a hangi as a cake.

HUA TŌTARA - TŌTARA BERRIES

The red flesh of the tōtara berries is eaten in autumn. They are tiny but tasty.

KAKAHA - MOUNTAIN ASTELIA – BERRIES

Sweet, orange berries in clusters. Eaten in late summer to autumn

KAREAO

Supplejack also known as the karewao is a black cane-like vine that twists among the forest trees. The red flesh of the kareao berrie are edible, as are the young vine shoots which appear in summer.

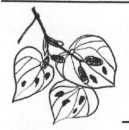

KAWAKAWA

Kawakawa leaves are used to make a herbal tea by steeping the leaves in boiling water. The leaves that caterpillars choose to chew are thought to be the best. The small ripe orange fruit can be eaten in summer, but are full of annoying tiny seeds.

MIRO BERRIES

Miro berries are reddish pink and are edible. Kereru feed on the ripe berries in autumn and early winter. The oil from the miro berry was used to repel pesky insects.

UREURE – KIEKIE FRUIT
TAWHARA – KIEKIE BRACTS

The fruit of the kiekie vine, ureure, ripen in autumn. Inside the knobbly pink fruit is an edible sweet pulp. The kiekie bracts or tawhara are considered a delicacy. They are eaten in spring.

TOI – MOUNTAIN CABBAGE TREE

The young shoots of the toi are said to be less bitter than those of ti kouka, the cabbage tree. They can be eaten raw or cooked.

TOETOE

The young shoots are edible. Also the stem can be chewed to extract a sugary flavour.

WHARARIKI – MOUNTAIN FLAX, COASTAL FLAX

The gum found at the base of the leaves was sometimes chewed by Maori.

SURVIVAL TIPS

What can you do to increase your chances of surviving and being found when lost in the bush?

1. Prepare

Make sure someone knows where you are going and when you expect to be back. If possible ensure you have a survival pack with you. This should contain: a waterproof bag containing a wet-weather coat or jacket, a warm jersey and hat (consider one of these being in a bright colour that can be easily seen), a whistle, basic medical kit, torch, bottled water and snacks.

2. Stay calm

When you realise you are lost stay calm. Try deep breathing. You'll think more clearly and make better decisions if you are calm.

3. Stay together

If you are in a group stay together.

4. Stay put

Remember the further you go the harder it will be to find you so stay put.

5. Make noise

Shout or, if you have one, blow your whistle. Continue doing this regularly.

6. Shelter

Make or find shelter and keep warm.

7. Find water

You will probably find water at the bottom of a gully so pay attention to the terrain and listen for the sound of running water.

8. Leave signs

If you have to move (to find shelter or water) leave an indication that you were there and where you are going. A pile of stones, a mark on a tree or, if these are not possible, dig the ground to make a deep mark indicating your direction.

GLOSSARY

These definitions are as the words are used in the context of this story.

āe	yes	namu	sandfly
aihe	dolphin	ngā	the (plural)
aue	a cry	Pākehā	European New Zealander
e	slang for 'don't you see?' Pronounced like ear.	Papatūanuku	Earth Mother
		pēpē	baby
e noho	sit down	pikau	backpack
haere mai	come here, welcome	pipi	a small shellfish
hāngī	food steamed in an earth oven	pōwhiri	opening ceremony, welcome
hapū	subtribe	piwakawaka	fantail
harakeke	flax	puku tawai	dried fungus fire starter
heke	rafter	Ranginui	Sky Father
hīnaki	eel-pot	tāhuhu	ridgepole
iti	small	tama	son, boy, child
iwi	tribe	Tangaroa	Maori guardian of the sea
ka kite anō	see you again	tapu	sacred
ka pai	good	tāwhara	the bract of the kiekie
kahawai	a saltwater fish	te	the (singular)
kakaha	astelia	tere haere	hurry
kai	food	tikanga Māori	Maori custom
kai moana	sea food	tōī	mountain cabbage tree
karakia	prayer	tokotoko	walking stick
karanga	call	tumeke	'awesome', superb
kaumātua	elders	tuna	eel
kererū	wood pigeon	tūpuna	ancestors
kete	flax basket	tūrangawaewae	home place
kia ora	hello, thanks	ureure	the fruit of the kiekie
kōrero	talk	waiata	song
koro	old man, grandfather	wairua	spirit
kōtiro	girl	waka	canoe
kūtai	mussel	wero	challenge
marae	meeting area and its buildings	whakapapa	genealogy
		whānau	family
mimi	urinate	whare	house
moko	short for mokopuna, grandchild	whare tupuna	meeting house
		whenua	land
mōrena	morning	whetū	star

ABOUT THE AUTHOR

Liz van der Laarse lives in the Far North and has taught in area and primary schools for many years.

She has had two middle fiction books previously published: *Trouble Patch* and *Not Even. Not Even* (2003) and *Cuz* (2019) received a Storylines Notable Book Award in the Junior Fiction category. It has been used as a class set by intermediate and junior secondary teachers.

Her titles have been reviewed by Jabberwocky, the New Zealand Listener, Brat, Magpies, the NZ Herald. and Kids Books.